Till Life Us Do Part

A Swedish best-seller, this scarifying book is the story of a marriage that has slipped, over twenty years, from romantic happiness, through slovenly toleration, into a preoccupation with plans for actual murder.

Told almost entirely in the private thoughts of the man and woman, the story strikes with a snake-like impact which can be terrifying. For those thoughts are common enough. Most married men and women will have had them—if only momentarily. To see them set down in black and white, professionally arranged into a real and ingenious plot, backed by a remarkable honesty of writing, and rammed through to the inevitable and logical end is to experience something which bursts in the mind with explosive recognition and a fine sense of horror.

A brilliant and original book.

Till Life Us Do Part

Elisabet Peterzén

Translated from the Swedish by
Marianne Kold Madsen

ALLAN WINGATE
LONDON & NEW YORK

First published in Great Britain
in Demy Octavo MCMLXX
by

Allan Wingate (Publishers) Ltd
14 Gloucester Road, SW7
and 235 E 45th Street
New York City

SBN 85523 002 9

Made and printed in Great Britain by
The Garden City Press Limited, Letchworth, Hertfordshire

1

I'M WAITING. I have plenty of time to wait. Years ahead of me like those gone by. I hardly feel them pass; they are so much the same. The room I'm sitting in is the same, the garden outside is the same. The same routine; getting up every morning in the dark or maybe seeing the white mist clinging to the ground. Sometimes the sun; yes, the sun, far away, leering at me like a rotten tomato—just like *him*, when I turn towards him in bed. His face red and rough from pimples he tried to squeeze out in his youth. His skin rough and leathery, red and chapped. Beard-stubble: never a proper beard. Never quite clean-shaven; always stubble, and that sour smell. I'm reluctant to turn in his direction.

How long have I been waiting? How many years have passed? I dare not begin to count them, for then I might start thinking about the past. My thoughts wander and come to a halt by the window, never venturing outside: just stop there, observing figures moving beyond the dirty windowpane—almost like looking through a slaughter-house window. Perhaps the sun shines on the other side. Perhaps there was sunshine once. I don't want to open the window. I don't want to see and remember. This is where I am now, and it is here that something must happen.

I get up—I always get up first! Always me first—and I drag myself down to the kitchen to make his breakfast.

I still get his meals! A little innocent poison—a pinch of arsenic, a little hydrocyanic acid, oh, so easy! He would collapse at lunchtime, blood running out of his mouth, or perhaps he would hang over his plate, his face purple and his tongue poking out. A little arsenic; a little hydrocyanic acid. Which I haven't got. And afterwards I'll still be here, alone with him till they come and ask, 'Why doesn't he come?' 'Is he ill?' 'Where is he?' It's no good; it's been done before. I must dig a deep grave in the garden sometime; I'll drag him there by his feet, his head dangling on the ground, and when I've put him into it, I'll cover it with earth—or better still, manure, so he'll be in his natural environment. Later, I'll plant flowers. Sunflowers first, to thank the sun for having let my world be light again. Gladioli, tall, proud, straight plants, heavy with flowers. Sunflowers and gladioli. No white lilies; they are the flowers of sorrow, and I shan't feel sorrow that day.

But they'll come. Then I'll have to say he's gone away, that he left suddenly and I don't know when he'll be back. But they'll look at me suspiciously and I'll know that they're thinking there's only one place he can be. They'll search. There won't be any poison left for them to find but they'll search the garden. . . .

I'm dreaming. When he's gone at last I'll go back to bed and straighten out his sheets to make it look as though he never lay there, so that I can feel completely alone. I'll never get up again. A spell of solitude, the richest happiness on earth. It'll be ages before I'll feel like getting up, and from then on time will be mine. I'll walk through the house once more on light feet; I'll open the window fully at last and let the light from outside reach me.

Never again shall I be sickened at hearing his steps outside in the hall—a sound that makes me shrink, makes my whole body writhe as though I have been kicked in the guts. He's here and I'm kneeling on the doormat, I'm an extension of the doormat, and I'm his obedient slave; 'Yes master', 'No master', and he laughs and plants a boot right in my face; he knows how much I detest him and he plays on it. It's like teasing a monkey behind bars—that's how he feels when he comes home to me in the evenings. He holds up a banana, the monkey stretches to reach it, obediently and greedily, and he pulls the banana back and stuffs it in his own mouth; laughing scornfully, he takes a bite, eats slowly. A stream of saliva dribbles down his chin, and the monkey rears in its cage, wild with fury and childish vexation. The monkey smashes itself against the cage and shows its teeth—long, yellow teeth —shakes the bars and shrieks horribly. That's how he sees me.

To be free to get up whenever I choose, to go to my wardrobe and to dress as I like. To choose, feel, let my hands run gently over the materials. I'll have beautiful clothes then, soft, fluffy wools. I'll dress in front of the mirror as I did before . . . before he came. I'll dress slowly and smile at my own reflection, change, undress, and put on something new. I'll go to the garden leaving the door wide open behind me; I'll walk slowly towards the grave and bend down to look at the flowers that grow around me.

The air light and warm, a bee will be humming above me but it won't sting me. I'll raise my hands towards the sun and let the warmth permeate me, fill me till I grow young, new, and pure again.

'Alone.' 'Solitude.' The words pass over my tongue like caresses. Oh, that my burden may remain heavy, get even heavier, so that my solitude may be so much the sweeter.

Thoughts, plans. They swarm through my head like flies in a glass, leaving a dark spot here and there. It's so wonderful lying here dreaming. Ways . . . means . . . I taste them, suck them, and spit them out again when exhausted. Time is my friend, I'm in no hurry. Every morning when I wake and see him lying there next to me, snoring and open-mouthed, I know that this day could be the last.

Once when I was young, I sat next to him in the twilight. There was no one else in the world. A light rain was falling, a drizzle, but it didn't bother us; it only enhanced the richness of the moment, of our caresses and the feeling that we were one. We said nothing; we expressed our feelings through our hands and bodies; too afraid to speak and let our ugly human voices disrupt the spell that surrounded us. That was us, it really was us then; but before we had been trapped by time, routine, worries, and tiredness; by having to look at the same old face growing older, rougher, and ever more ugly. . . .

Oh, I have so many plans. I read so many books—all the books I can get. I read the newspapers, but I feel that the odds are against me.

A murder is often committed and the murderer goes free, an unknown murderer, laughing inside; frightened at first, perhaps, lest somebody might guess—might realise; but slowly the fear is absorbed and becomes a small part of his everyday life, and in the end he doesn't feel it at all. So often the murderer goes free and nobody knows where or who he is. He arrives, softly and quietly, strikes and goes away again; but that doesn't apply to me.

I have read enough to know that only when the murderer is a stranger does he get away unseen; seldom when the murdered person was related to him. No, they have so many tricks and traps, and they always guess; more often than not they know right from the beginning that only one person could have done it. To think that I could go out in the streets and kill a child and nobody would ever suspect me; besides women never kill children, it's always men. But if *he* died, who would they ask first, if not me. The sorrowing widow! —and they'd soon detect from my eyes and my bearing that I was not mourning as sincerely as expected. They would nod to each other and then trap me with all their questions.

No, no, I'll have to be smarter than all of them. I must think, plan; perhaps for years before I find the one way, the right way. The time I waste now I'll have back a hundredfold afterwards. That's why I'm still waiting, silently.

2

HELL AND damnation. It looks as though these windows
have never been cleaned. Covered in dirt and muck; and
those dead plants that just hang there dangling down on
to the radiator. This damned mess everywhere, this
slovenliness, this filth.

As though the slut had anything else to do. As though
the slut *ever* had to do anything else than look after
me, make life comfortable for me. Who should she thank
for living here? Who has she got to thank for having a
house to live in, windows to clear? It's hell with this
creature. So loving before she was married! So eager to
please! Nothing was too good for me, nothing too much
trouble! 'As you like, my darling, you decide.' She wore
the smartest little numbers and undressed with style; she
spent hours over her hair and make-up; she would press
herself against me, smelling of beautiful scents, put her
arm under mine. There was nothing she wouldn't do,
nothing she wouldn't give.

There was a time when she was more than human,
when she was divine; when she was a being of flesh and
blood—not this flabby mountain of fat, white, bulging
and loose. I wish I were a piraya fish in a South
American river and that she would come down to my
river and have a dip. Then I would tear that flesh of
hers, see the blood running, tear and pull, ask all my

brothers to eat. Look at her lying there. Fat, loose and flabby and without a thought in her head, the lank, thin hairs greasy and shiny on the pillow, her blotchy cheeks and sunken mouth. Did I ever want to touch this flesh? All those promises. When she said, 'Oh, I'll always be the way you like me, my darling, always please you. You can have me as often as you like, when and where you like; on the grass in public if you like, my darling.' Dinner ready and a kiss at the door, and tidy clean clothes. Sunday walks arm in arm; 'That's my woman, she doesn't look at all bad.' She promised all the way to the altar. There she stood radiant like the sun while I, the ox, the great, stupid, slow ox, didn't realise that I was trapped then, on my way to the slaughter-house. How I have paid for my stupidity!

I remember her confident smile at the wedding reception, after she had taken off her shoes under the table to air her crumpled toes, when she said to her friend across the table: 'Yes, now I'm married so I needn't bother any more!' She turned to me and pressed my hand as she said it, looking at me in that special way. But I should have known then that she was speaking the truth.

God, if I were free again. A free man, no longer burdened by this flesh by my side. If I could wake in the mornings and open the window and let in the fresh air, sing in the bathroom and not have to know that she was shrinking under the sheets, pulling them over her head. If I could go down and eat breakfast without having to see her sleepy face across the table. Make the coffee myself, strong and hot and good, the way I like it, and not have her eternal dish-water 'it's good for the heart'—whose bloody heart?—just because she will insist on playing the martyr and stumbling down to get my breakfast. Oh, if only she would stay in bed, stay there, for God's sake, so I didn't have to look at her.

If only she could get some damned crippling disease so I could get rid of her, somewhere out of my sight, be free to get the bottle out on Saturday evenings without having to see her pained face and know what she expected from me afterwards! To be rid of this ritual every Saturday, be rid of this flabby flesh!

To be alone! To close my eyes and think of nice women with firm bodies, women who undress slowly piece by piece and show me what they've got, and let me feel it; big shapely breasts that don't hang like bags of potatoes, a stomach that's part of the body. In my dreams they stand in front of me, show me everything. They lie down and let me look, before they slowly come up to me and put my hands on their bodies. I could go to town then, and get women—women who know the art.

I close my eyes and pretend to be asleep for soon she'll get up and put her corn-infested feet into those old, worn-out slippers and stand and breathe filth over me, saying in nagging voice, 'Get up! Get up! You must get up!'

3

"GET UP! Get up! You must get up!"

Always the same drudgery. Always the same rigmarole before he at last gets out of bed.

"I'm awake. Leave me alone. Go away. I am awake."

"Well, make sure you get out of bed then, you drunkard. How do you think you can get up in the mornings when you sit up all night drinking? I don't know how late it was last night before. . . ."

"No, you don't know and it's none of your business either! Leave me alone, I know when to get up—at least let me stay in bed till you get out of here. Why don't you make coffee or do something useful instead of just standing there jabbering?"

"So that's all the thanks I get. The thanks for being the only one who cares about you, so much that I even worry about getting you up in the mornings. If it wasn't for me you'd lie in bed all day."

"And if it wasn't for me you probably wouldn't have anybody to wake up—you'd be a sour, bitter old cow whom nobody liked and you'd be forced to *work for a living*! Bear that in mind."

"Bear that in mind. Bear that in mind," she muttered while her slippers went shambling towards the door. He decided not to have a nap and opened his eyes when he heard her halfway down the stairs.

Then he started moving and breathed deeply a couple

13

of times. He might as well have gone on sleeping, but getting up in the mornings had become a habit just like everything else.

He rubbed his face and his armpits while he stood on the mat by the bed, yawned widely and felt his penis. There it hung, small and floppy. Still, it was there.

He stalked into the bathroom and ran the water, dabbed his face with cold water, took the razor and started to soap his face. His eyes looked back sourly at him from the mirror. At least you look like a man. You deserve a better woman than the one you've got. You really ought to do something about it, damn it! A razor in her throat—oh, that's so easy! An accident— 'I'm sorry, I just wanted to give the little wife a hug and I completely forgot that I had the razor in my hand. How unfortunate! I'm sorry, I didn't mean to!'

He laughed gruffly and finished shaving. By the time he had got dressed and got down to the kitchen she had put two cups on the table and stood leaning against the sink watching the coffee while it filtered. A couple of slices of bread were lying on a chipped plate next to a packet of margarine.

"I've told you time and time again that I want butter on my bread," he grumbled.

"All right, you want butter. But you'll have to buy it yourself, my little man. Considering the amount of money you give me you ought to be glad that we've even got margarine. Do you really think that there's enough for butter as well in this house?"

He sat down and made a sandwich in silence.

"Haven't we got any cheese either?"

She sighed heavily, carried the coffee pot to the table, walked to the fridge and produced a wedge of cheese.

"Here you are. There's marmalade too if you really want to spoil yourself."

He shrugged his shoulders.

She sat down opposite him and poured out a cup of coffee for herself.

"You know what . . ." he began.

She looked at him.

Their eyes met.

4

HE'S GONE. He's gone at last and I can sit down and drink my coffee in peace and quiet as I like it, without having to be on the alert and listen to his remarks and new demands. He just leaves everything on the table, wouldn't even dream of putting his cup on the draining board. Breadcrumbs all over the tablecloth where he's been sitting. 'After all you haven't got anything else to do except look after me.' I've got all day to brush away his eternal breadcrumbs. Yes, of course. After that I'll have to make the beds too, and try to straighten his tangled sticky sheet. My bed is always nice and tidy when I get up in the morning. But his! Twisted, crumpled, sticky sheets and black bits of God knows what at the foot end. But as I said, I haven't anything else to do, after all.

When I have made the beds, I sit down by the kitchen table with pen and paper. I suppose he thinks that I haven't got enough brains to write or even anything to write about! But my head is full of plans. I once read somewhere about ground glass. You take some very brittle glass and grind it, in a mortar for instance, and mix the powder with something drinkable. How easy it would be. I take a small, thin liqueur glass and break it against the table—like this—and wipe up the bits and pieces and put them in the mortar and I take the pestle and grind the bits very conscientiously until it becomes powder, white powder, almost transparent. I mix it with the coffee, it's hardly noticeable, just like small undissolved sugar grains. He won't notice.

I put them at the bottom of his coffee cup and hand it to him—after all, it's much too much bother for him to reach for it himself—and then he drinks. The pains won't come immediately. He goes out and I won't have to watch when it happens. I'll stay here, make myself a sandwich and after a while I'll turn on the radio. I'll listen to the music and the songs about love and youth and finally the phone rings, I go to answer it : 'Your husband has fallen seriously ill, some kind of ulcer, so please hurry before it is too late.' Let us sincerely hope it will be too late. I won't want to see his eyes then for he will have realised, as soon as the pains start he will understand and know that I was more cunning than he thought. 'My dear, dear husband.' I take his weak, cold hand and press it against my breast and begin to sob : 'Why did this have to happen to us? We were so happy! My dear, you mustn't leave me, not yet, we should have so many years left together. . . .' I weep and throw myself on him, kiss him and try to bring him back to life; finally, they have to carry me out of the room. I am overwhelmed by this inexplicable, horrifying thing. 'How could it have happened? He seemed perfectly normal this morning when he left home. He was absolutely healthy, what can have happened, how did it happen?'

The scene is perfect up to this point, but it won't stop here. I have to reject this method, for there must have been a reason why he died, and they'll find that when they open his stomach. How could he have got glass into his stomach? . . . They'll ask questions, the sorrowing widow will be attacked from every direction and the clue points only one way.

Well, it was a good idea, she thought, but went to the sink, poured out the bits of glass and washed up the breakfast cups.

Then there are fish that can go off if they're kept in the tin, some kind of poison develops in the tin, and you haven't got many chances against that if you've eaten enough of it. I made a bulk purchase when it had been reported in the papers. He had tinned salmon right, left and centre for several weeks. Small puddings and pies, God help me, and fresh from the tin and in salads every now and again—only he seldom touches salads 'It's so very cheap these days,' I tried to explain, 'you get it even cheaper if you buy in bulk, and besides it contains so many useful vitamins'—or was it protein? never mind—'tinned fish is essential.'

He ate the muck for quite a while, but of course I had got hold of the wrong kind. It was a chance in a million. I had never really thought it would work. But if it had I would have been an inconsolable widow and nobody would have asked me any questions.

God, if he knew about my little book! I have collected all the possibilities that I've thought of so far; when I read something interesting in the paper I cut it out and stick it in my wonderful little scrap-book. There are recipes, together with all kinds of accidents that can happen in and out of the home; anything that can kill a man is entered. But of course it'll have to look like an accident. Like when he was going to help me clean the windows.

'It's such a shame that the top windows open outwards and that I suffer so terribly from dizziness. It isn't my fault and I really can't do anything about it, so please yourself; the windows won't be cleaned unless you help me do them. God, I get so dizzy when I hang on to the window frame and see the yard down below. Yes, I know that plenty of people get over it and think nothing of it, that it's foolishness, but I can't help it if I get dizzy; that's how it is. You're either like that or you aren't. You should be grateful that you don't suffer like me. A window-cleaner? What nonsense when I have a strong, healthy man in the house.' Well, he had to admit that it would be a rather unnecessary expense.

Up on the window sill he climbed, the old man with cloths and spray by his side. Poor little wife stayed inside by the window, all squeamish and squawking. 'The top corner as well; that's where all the dirt gathers and if you don't get rid of that . . . surely you can reach a little higher'—and at the same time the poor wife noticed that the bottle of spray was about to fall off the window sill, and what could the poor woman do except reach down to try and save it before it fell on to the floor where it would have made a nasty big mark on the carpet—knowing what a fuss he would have made had it happened, and who knows whether stuff like that can ever be removed? I was quite simply forced to save the bottle. Out went husband and cloth and everything. It was a ghastly moment. He was squealing like a pig. Then he went quiet, in fact he had concussion and two broken ribs, and he fainted for a few moments after the fall. The little wife stood beside him wringing her hands.

Neighbours and all sorts of other people rushed up to him; it wasn't long before the doctor came and bandaged him. He had to stay in bed for a fortnight and the poor little wife had to run about and look after him day and night, fetching all the medicine he needed and tobacco and papers with crossword puzzles. And I had to listen to the sports news on the radio, never any music; oh yes, he knew how to get his revenge! He could have tried to make life a little easier for me, since I had all the bother; but no, he just lay there like a king, thriving on it, swearing and carrying on worse then ever. Just changing the sheets under that heavy pig. . . . I know who needed to be in bed for a fortnight after that ordeal.

I've never been able to make him clean the windows again. He simply refuses to do it ('You won't get a chance to push me out again, you bitch', he says, but really he's wrong because it *was* an accident), and I won't clean them either; I get dizzy and if he's too mean to pay a window-cleaner to do it, well then the windows will just have to stay dirty. Damn it, one can hardly see through them. I don't quite remember how long ago all that nonsense happened, but it must be a long time. And I'm not going to be the one to give in and clean them just for the sake of peace and quiet. They'll have to stay dirty till he gets round to asking a window-cleaner to come.

5

"ARE YOU at home?" he shouted as he came in at the front door.

No answer.

"Are you at home?"

He tore off his hat and coat and put down his briefcase on the table in the hall.

"Where are you?"

Still no answer.

Damn! Damn! Not even that. All day she's got, not a thing to do in the house that couldn't be done in half an hour. She goes shopping, yes I admit that, but surely women do that in the mornings. They ought to tidy up too. But not her, oh no. She'll lie in bed as long as possible and read rubbishy muck and write things on little bits of paper. And she's got a scrap-book hidden away somewhere. He'd have a look at that one day. Secrets! Probably she thought they were things he was too stupid to understand. No doubt she was sitting somewhere now fiddling with all her secret bits and pieces as though she had all the time in the world, as though she had nothing else to think about but herself.

He went into the kitchen. At least the washing up had been done, but there was no food on the cooker, nor in the oven, and the table hadn't been laid.

"Where the hell are you?" he cried, slamming his fist

on the table to release some of his fury although she wasn't in the room—it would be her turn later.

He walked over to the fridge, took out butter and some herrings—butter? margarine, damn it!—and then went to the cupboard to get himself a glass. 'You drink too much. Don't sit up drinking all night and every night. Don't you ever want to go to bed? You're just sitting there drinking without a thought for me who's been slaving all day. . . .' He emptied the glass with a satisfied look on his face.

He went into the living room, and there she was. She was either so engrossed in what she was doing or she was pretending not to notice him, just to upset him. He took a deep breath in readiness for another shout, swallowed the air and stood looking at her. She was sitting at the small bureau in the corner, bent over some papers; she was wearing a dress instead of her dressing-gown but the slippers were still on her feet and her stockings were hanging round her ankles. She didn't turn her head to look at him. Perhaps she really hadn't heard him?

He stayed by the door breathing slowly; opening and closing his hands. Her neck was bent forward so that the vertebra was visible, and her hair was held to the sides with pins. He slowly took one step forward, moved one foot into the room and let the other follow without a sound. He was forced to put a hand across his mouth in order to conceal the sound of his breathing, tried to breathe through his nose instead. One more step. And another. As though standing beside himself observing the scene, he saw a smile playing on his face, saw how at last he smiled at her, the first time for—how long?

I needn't do it. I mustn't do it right now. It isn't the

22

right moment. To make it look natural, I would have to sneak out again and then come in looking for her, find her and burst into loud shouts and roars. But it wouldn't stand the test. They would examine her later and then they would find that death had occurred at a time when he was already home, or ought normally to have been home. It wouldn't stand up. Why hadn't he seen the murderer? Had he noticed anything. Hadn't he seen anybody come or go? Was there another man? Another man, her? A laugh bubbled up inside him but he forced it back between his teeth, back into his throat again. Perhaps some day just after he had been paid his wages. All the money in the house gone. Things broken to pieces, drawers opened, clothes spread all over the floor. There would have to be a gun or a heavy iron bar or an iron. Perhaps an iron. . . .

But then strangulation, choking from behind, wouldn't be the right method. The thought was settling within him. He would carry it with him, consider it, let it ripen in his subconscious with all the other ideas.

The idea about a car. The car that backed out when she stood by the gate to see if the postman was on his way. The idea about them walking one Sunday and her suddenly slipping and falling into the road just as a car went past.

The idea about her falling from the steps of the bus just as it started, and the back wheels. . . . Difficult ideas. Difficult.

Or when the car went off the road because he had fallen asleep at the wheel and suddenly woke up. The seat next to the driver's is the most dangerous one. He hadn't seen the tree by the road because he had fallen asleep and she, who should have helped keep him awake, had forgotten her duty as usual and fallen asleep herself or just sat there staring, sour and nasty without wanting to talk to him since all their recent quarrels.

But this. Her bent neck, bony and sharp. How can anybody have such a bony neck and still be so fat further down? Step by step he walked silently over the carpet, stopping after each step, opening his hands, rubbing them together without realising it.

Holding his breath he stood behind her and looked at the open book in front of her.

". . . youths killed by exhaust fumes," he read.

6

WHEN HE had read enough he raised his hands and put them softly round her neck. He started pressing, not very hard, while letting his hands slide up and down her neck.

She cackled like a frightened hen while she fought to get up; her arms were swinging helplessly in the air, but he held her tight.

"What an interesting book you've got there. 'Youths killed by exhaust fumes in a car', I see. Wouldn't you like to go for a ride in the car with your husband? How about a ride, eh?"

Her hand fell on to the book, closing it with an automatically protective gesture which the shock of his grip had prevented earlier.

He let his fingers press yet again, let them press for longer, let them sink in deeper, pressing harder and harder. Then he let go of her and stepped aside, observing with interest her attempt to regain her self-possession.

Words were fighting in her throat but couldn't get out; her face was red, her eyes stood out. She pressed the book to her bosom, shaking and looked as though she was about to be sick.

"What's in that book of yours?" he asked in a friendly voice, taking a step towards her, his arms stretched out in front of him.

She stepped backwards, hugging the book, and as she tried to get her voice under control she actually managed to spit.

"You!" she finally shouted. "Now I know. You're absolutely mad! Attempted murder, that's what it is!" She began to cry.

"Now, now, don't cry, little wife, you must know that I was only joking," he answered in a friendly voice. "Now let me have that book so that I can take a look at it too."

Her eyes scanned the walls and the distance to the door, but she stood still clutching the book to her.

"It's so sad when young people die," he said, "so very sad."

"I'll go to the police!" she cried. "It was attempted murder, you think I don't know. I know what you go around thinking. You wish I were dead," she shouted. "I work and slave to make a nice home for you and I have to put up with all your tricks and nastiness and this is the thanks I get—you try to murder *me,* your own wife." She started to cry, her face already distorted by tears and shouting. It was ugly, furious crying which reddened her face even more and made her wrinkles deeper.

He sat down in a chair, smiling in a friendly manner. He had the situation under control, he knew it, he had her in his power now; he had observed her and let her feel his fingers; she knew that he had her where he wanted her and that he knew what she had been doing.

"You must give me that book to read later," he went on softly.

"It's my book! Never! I'd sooner burn it!"

26

He got up from the chair very slowly and came towards her.

"You'll give me that book just the same. I'm sure there must be things in it that I, too, would like to read."

She turned round and tried to run past him to get out but he stood between her and the door. He stretched his hands out. "You'd better give it to me. If you don't I'll get it anyway. You can be sure of that. I'll get hold of it somehow."

His raised voice betrayed that his fury had returned, the fury he had buried deep inside him while he had walked up behind her, reading over her shoulder and letting his fingers play with her neck.

"So this is what you do during the day," he exploded. "You damned bitch. I knew you were sour and miserable, but to go so far as to plan to murder your own husband—why, you wouldn't even have a bed to sleep in if it weren't for me!"

His anger welled up inside him and for a moment clouded his vision; red shadows played before his eyes.

"Give me that book! Give it to me, and get out of my house, you bloody bitch, and don't ever come back as long as I'm here. Get out! Get out!"

She weighed him up, watching him cunningly as he shouted; this was a tone of voice she knew, now she was on a par with him and could defend herself.

"Just you try! Try! Try! Haven't I ever got the right to do what I want when you aren't at home? Can't I even have any interests of my own. Oh, no, I'm supposed to look after you day and night while you do nothing but plan how you can kill me. That's the

27

thanks I get; that's why I've been slaving for you for all these years. . . ."

He walked up to her and twisted her arms backwards so that he could grab the book. She tried to reach for it but he got away. "Thanks," he said, "and now for God's sake get some food on the table while I have a rest. Get on with it, or do you want me to stand behind you telling you what to do? Do you want me to stand behind you like this and. . . ."

She fled to the kitchen screaming.

7

"Aaah," he said slowly. "I see."

She didn't answer. She hadn't said a word since he had taken the book away from her. She had gone to the kitchen, red-eyed, tight lipped, now and again snorting through her nose, but she hadn't said a word. She banged loudly with crockery and saucepans, dropped a couple of knives on the floor, broke some glasses. To her surprise he didn't utter one word about her clumsiness; he smiled mildly and had settled down in the kitchen to watch while she cooked the dinner; he had brought the book with him and sat on it—his triumph was both mild and enormous.

"Ah yes, little woman," he said occasionally, "I see."

She fried a couple of slices of sausage and some old potatoes, tossed them on to his plate, but took nothing herself.

"Isn't there a beer for me today?" he asked sweetly.

With a glance at him over her shoulder she took a few steps towards the fridge. She came to a halt, opened her mouth as though to say something but closed it again with a sigh before any words reached her lips. She took a bottle and put it on the table before him with a bang.

"Ah, my beer, thank you."

With her hands on her hips she stood looking at him, hatred in her glance. Power! Power was what he was feeling. He thought he had the upper hand now, but did he really think he could enslave her just because he had seen her book? What was in that book to justify him in suppressing her like this, and for God knows how long? There was nothing in it. Criminal cases. Descriptions of various murders. A few remarks she had added herself. But nothing, nothing that could put her in a spot. Nothing that he could show to somebody else that would endanger her. And then? 'I'm living such a narrow and boring life, a prisoner in this rotten house, alone all day, nothing to do but look after him, surely I'm allowed a hobby. A little insignificant hobby, all my own.'

It would have been different if he had discovered she had a lover; then he could have stared at her like that, sly and revengeful. A lover! If only she had! Or if she had really tried to kill him. He would then have had a reason for that supercilious, triumphant expression. It was she who ought to look at him instead. She still felt them, the spots where he had squeezed her neck, how swollen and sore and red they were. Big marks from his fingers. She could get him sent to jail for that. She could go to the police about it and get rid of him for a good while. It was she who had him in a spot.

He shoved the bottle towards her.

"Pour out some for me."

"Do it yourself if you want some," she said. "You pander to your own alcoholic habits."

He stared back at her.

"I said. . . ."

"I heard what you said. Go and get your own drink."

"You'd better be careful, my dear. You really must be nice and kind to your husband tonight and make it comfortable for him when he sits down to read."

"I suppose you think I'm afraid of you?" she snorted.

"And why not? It isn't exactly fairy tales you've collected in this book."

"I collect what I like. I've got a right to my hobby and when you never bother about me, then. . . ."

He slammed his fist on the table making the beer bottle bounced.

"Now, you and I are going to have a serious talk," he roared. "Don't try to tell me that you collect things like this just for fun. There's obviously a plan behind all this in your muddled bird brain, stupid though you are, you probably thought that you could. . . ."

"Could! Are you really so sure I'd want to get rid of you? Do you really think yourself you're so bad that it's the only thing I could do?"

She leaned over the table, her hands clutching the edge.

"You and your sick, dirty, filthy imagination. You sly, sneaky little murderer. There I was, not suspecting any mischief, reading a little, amusing myself with my hobby and then you came from behind—I can still feel it. You tried to kill me, you did! There I was, sitting reading, completely innocent and not hurting a fly; as though it isn't my right to have a little relaxation after I've been slaving for you all day, I'm sitting there all innocent reading and studying my book and then you come sneaking over the carpet so that I can't hear you, and you, you try to strangle me. Talk about *my* sinister plans! Attempted murder, that's what it was and don't try to deny it. I can feel it still! I can hardly breathe. I can feel I'm swollen. I could go to the police right away and how far do you think you'd get with your little book then, how much do you think that'd be worth?"

He sat in silence for a while. His hand lay flat on the table. She bent towards him even further and jutted her jaw triumphantly. Spirit had returned to her eyes again.

"Do you really think you could accuse me of anything and get away with it? After they had seen the marks on my neck?"

He lifted his hand from the table and felt instinctively under his collar. He glanced around him. She stood there holding on to the edge of the table, laughing.

"Think of something better," she said, "just you go ahead and read. Then maybe you can think of something better for when you try next time."

He sat absolutely still, slack-jawed.

"You didn't answer my question," he said finally in a quiet, somewhat distant voice. "How long have you been doing this? You really do sit there thinking that you'd get away with murdering me, don't you?"

She snorted loudly.

He rose up from the chair and took out the book from under him, pushed the plate with the uneaten food away from him, put the book on the table and began to turn the pages.

"There's something here about potassium cyanide," he said. "It says that bitter almonds contain potassium cyanide. Somebody has written in the margin that twenty bitter almonds, eaten within a short while. . . ."

"Yes, and what's wrong with that. I'm interested in criminal cases."

He went on turning the pages.

"Old Christie, you've got him here too. The one

32

• •

who shoved little bits under the floor boards. Not a very good method for you, eh? It would soon stink the place out and you wouldn't be able to excuse it with your bad hygiene. 'Oh, what's that stink in your kitchen, could it be your husband by any chance?' "

"Oh yes," she muttered, "I know what's stinking in my kitchen all right."

"And what about this then? Suitcase murder!" He laughed heartily. "Have you had the axe sharpened lately? The lady took her bag and went out. . . .'"

"There you are; see how stupid it sounds. If I were to kill you do you really think I'd do it that way? You really haven't got much brains. Accusing me of planning a suitcase murder!"

"Hell, what about this then. You've written this yourself. Overdose of medicines, possibilities: digitalis, sleeping pills, nerve tablets, insulin. . . . And what about this! Surgical spirit!"

She looked down at the table again, twisting her fingers. She had sat down on the chair opposite him. Both were silent for a long while.

"We could of course always get a divorce," she said eventually, in a weak voice.

He laughed shortly.

"Thank you very much. Stand there in court and talk to the judge and have to listen to your nonsense and all your complaints, you bitch. Oh, yes, that would suit you fine of course, you could always try and ask for a divorce and then see how it goes. You're also welcome to think about who should move out of the house. I could tell them about the time when I cleaned the windows for you, for instance. I could always think of something to say so that a certain person would be left

33

without alimony and would have to find somewhere to live for herself and perhaps even have to *work*, ha ha."

She looked around her uneasily. Divorce? She would be rid of him but what would she get instead? Lose the house, lose her regular income, be forced to put up with people's laughter; perhaps they'd think he had another woman?—Him? Who would want to have anything to do with him?—And they'd talk about her and she'd have to start working; no longer able to lie in bed in the mornings after he'd gone to work. And what chances did she have of getting work at her age, except perhaps occasional jobs. And she couldn't stay in the house but would have to move. . . .

Laughter instead of the sincere sympathy and com- miseration to which she would be entitled as a grieving widow; 'how brave she was, living only for her husband, devoted herself entirely to her home. . . .' She wouldn't get any of his money either if they separated. Money, he probably didn't have very much . . . but he had put some in the bank; she didn't know how much . . . it could be several hundred, he was so mean with the housekeeping money, for he didn't gamble and he really only drank on Saturdays.

"No," she said, sighing. "You're right. There's no point in getting a divorce."

"I thought as much," he laughed. "Don't you start thinking I'd let you divorce me and I'm damned if I want to spend a lot of money getting a divorce myself. Oh no, I'll put up with things as they are. And there's not going to be any dividing up or going short for your sake. It's all mine, every bit of this house is mine."

"Not the book, that's mine. Give it back to me."

"Oh no. Oh no, not so easily."

34

"You can't do anything with it, anyway. It's me who can accuse you so don't sit there trying to be superior. You know I could have you put behind bars if I wanted to."

He leaned forward.

"I can't see any marks on your neck," he said in a friendly voice.

She quickly put a hand to her neck as though to protect it.

"I could go to the police anyway. I can say I'm afraid of living here with you."

"Of course you can, but what do you think they'd do? Come here and have a look at me? And what would they see? A man sitting eating his dinner, and they couldn't help thinking what a bloody awful dinner it was, and he'd say: 'Don't pay any attention to my wife, she's a bit soft in the head. Come on now dear, let's be friends and not worry about this any more. She's got some funny ideas, you see, Constable, just look at this book, this is what she fiddles with all day long—she's got murder on her brain!' Perhaps it wouldn't be *me* they took back to the station with them."

She sat wetting her lips and locking her fingers together.

"There is one thing," she said.

"What's that then?"

"You might as well admit it. I know you want me out of the way. Oh yes, I know all right, do you think I haven't known for a long time. I suppose you've been hoping to frighten the life out of me or torture me to death. But I'm tougher than you think. My courage doesn't fail me because of little things like that, I'll stick it out as long as you. Oh, no, don't contradict me. I *know* you want to get rid of me."

This time he didn't answer immediately, but waited for her to continue.

"And book or no book I can tell you that nothing would gladden me more than becoming a widow, and the sooner the better. Please don't think I'm happy living like this, getting beatings and hard words after all I've done for you. It was you who wanted to marry me but you haven't shown any gratitude at all, even though I left everything just to follow you. Don't think I didn't have other admirers, but it was you I chose . . . and this is the way you thank me."

It was impossible to tell whether her sobs were genuine or put on for effect.

"Well, you weren't exactly difficult to persuade—I know very well who was the more eager of us two. 'Please marry me, don't leave me, I want only you'," he peeped in a high-pitched voice.

She sat up straight.

"There is, of course, another way," she said without looking at him.

"And what would that be other than sending you to a beauty salon and that wouldn't do you much good, you old bag."

"Suicide."

8

"THANK YOU very much," he answered after a while then laughed heartily. "That wouldn't be at all a bad idea. Thank you very much indeed. It really is a generous offer. How would you do it? Did you think of hanging yourself in the broom-cupboard, or perhaps drowning in the bath? Pity we don't have gas, it seems to be so easy to stick one's head in the oven. . . ."

"I?" she said with a harsh laugh. "Who said I would commit suicide?"

She got up determinedly and moved the plate with his cold dinner on to the side table.

"Do you want your beer?" she asked in a friendly way. "Or shall I put it back in the fridge?"

He grabbed hold of the bottle as though it were a weapon.

"Then what the hell do you mean by suicide?"

She leaned nonchalantly against the kitchen table.

"I mean that *one* of us could commit suicide."

"Well, don't count on me to sacrifice myself," he snarled. "Just to do you a favour, I suppose?"

"Not exactly that," she went on softly. "I just thought that it would be possible to make it look like suicide, even if it wasn't. As you said about pills, for instance. Or drowning in the bath. Hanging in the broom-cupboard would of course be a trifle difficult to arrange, don't you think?"

37

She scraped the food into the dustbin and began to fill the sink with water for the washing up, checking that it was warm enough while looking at him over her shoulder. He moved about uneasily.

"What damn schemes have you been brewing up?"

"I haven't planned it yet," she said lightly. "I haven't really decided how to go about it. First of all, you see, there'll have to be a suicide letter."

"Exactly," he said, "and I'm not going to write one, you can be sure of that. Or did you think of forging my handwriting, perhaps?" He laughed noisily.

"No, no, you don't understand what I mean. You're going to write the letter yourself."

He laughed even louder.

"Just you laugh. But wait till you've heard it all." She shook the washing up water off her hands and came over to him.

"Like this," she whispered eagerly. "You write a letter, a real suicide letter, and you write it yourself. In return. . . ."

"Perhaps you were thinking of giving me a splendid funeral? Floods of tears at the grave?"

She shook her head.

"No, no. In return I write a suicide letter and give it to you."

He looked at her for a long time. Then he suddenly broke into a broad smile and nodded several times.

"You aren't so stupid! You really aren't so stupid!"

"Now you see what I mean. You write a letter and give it to me, and I write you a letter. That way we have one each—just in case." He continued to nod, as

38

though confirming something that he had already thought of.

"And what," he asked, "what makes you so sure that I'm going to give in first? It might just happen that. . . ."

"I know," she interrupted, "but if you try to do anything to me I can go to the police and show them your letter and tell them everything. I can tell them that it was all a joke, but that I now realise that you were serious."

"And what if I should succeed?"

"Well, it's up to each of us to be the first to succeed."

"Maybe . . . maybe . . ." she continued very softly, ". . . if we both had each other's letters we might not behave like this any more. If you know that I have your letter perhaps you'll be more careful and I . . . we could end all this. If we had them as a kind of safeguard, I mean."

He got up from his chair and put his arms round her shoulders for the first time in a long while.

"Who knows, maybe you're right, little woman. We haven't really been very pleasant to each other lately. Listen, we'll write these letters now, as you said, and then exchange them and hide them somewhere and forget all about them. Yes, we'll forget about all this. But we'll write the letters first so that we can remind each other if one of us should get these absurd thoughts like these again."

She turned towards him and they smiled at each other. Then she put her hands in her apron pockets and rubbed her cheek against his shoulder.

"That's just what I meant. We'll be all square, and

39

then we can stop being so silly and childish with one another."

He gave her behind a friendly slap.

"Now, my sweetie, let's have a glass of whisky; and then we'll sit down and write those letters and get the whole thing over and done with."

9

My DEAR, forgive me for what I'm doing. I can't go on any longer. Thanks for all these years we've had together and forgive me for having made you unhappy. I hope we'll meet again. Forgive me.

"Oughtn't there be something about why?" she asked.

"For Christ's sake, there is no more than one reason," he answered. "I can't stand living with you any longer, you cow, but that won't do, of course, it'll give them something to go by. They might think it wasn't suicide."

She snorted abruptly.

"I suppose it's the only thing you can say then. At least they won't think I wrote it, if we leave it like that."

"Then I'll put that down."

"No, you don't write like that, it doesn't sound right. It's like you to think of something so stupid."

They deliberated for some time.

"Well what do you suggest, then?" he asked.

"Money?" She studied him.

"Money, what do you know about my money? Do you expect me to say I'm bankrupt when I'm not. That isn't exactly clever."

"You could draw all your money out and have it at home instead of in the bank," she suggested slyly.

He roared with laughter.

"Oh yes. And leave you alone with it all day. That would be something! Anyhow, you can bet your life I'll be living it up with my money as soon as you are out of the way. So don't try to be clever with me."

"Well, what do we do, then. I don't like what we've got here."

"Depression," he suggested.

"Yes, of course, but so suddenly?"

"There is, of course, always that religious garble," he said.

"My Lord has summoned me, or something like that."

"H'mm." She bit the pen while shaking her head.

"I think I have suffered from a terrible disease, and I don't want to suffer and be a burden to you," he suggested.

"Yes, of course. But we can't both go to the doctor and complain about the same thing. A thing like that doesn't just appear out of thin air.

"In that case we can always use the world situation as an excuse," he said grimly. " 'In a world full of wars and famine. . . .' "

"Should we try that, do you think?"

"Let's."

They read it out again :

My dear, please forgive what I'm doing. I can't go on any longer. Thanks for all these years we've had together and forgive me for having made you un-happy. In a world full of wars and struggle I no long have the will to live. Forgive me.

"No, that's no good. It doesn't make sense."

"We could say it as it is. People often commit suicide

and others wonder afterwards what made them do it. 'He seemed so happy and satisfied with life', and so on; 'I don't understand why he did it.' "

"No, of course. But that's the kind who just do it without leaving a letter. If you leave a letter you'll have to say why you did it, not just vague hints like the world situation."

She tore the paper to bits.

"OK, you're always right. Why can't *you* think of something since you know so much."

"We needn't write exactly the same, you know," he said cautiously. "We could each write what we think best and then just exchange letters."

She looked at him suspiciously.

"How do I know that you. . . ."

"How do I know that *you'll* do it? It would be rather funny if both letters were fiddled."

"We'd better do that then. But I want to see your letter before I give you mine."

"O.K."

She ostentatiously turned her back and sat down to write by the sink.

"I'm ready now."

"Wait a minute. I haven't quite finished."

He had got up and stood waving his letter in the air while she went on writing.

"May I have a look now?"

"Wait, I haven't finished yet."

She bit her pen thoughtfully while her head nodded rhythmically.

"If you're going to sit here all night. . . ."

"How can I write with you standing there yapping all the time."

Finally she wrote a few sentences and looked up. "Ready."

"Let's have a look then."

They stood facing each other; one hand outstretched while they hid their own letters behind their backs.

"We'll put them beside each other on the table."

"I'd prefer to keep hold of mine, so that you can't grab it."

The letters now lay side by side on the table. They leered at each other.

"You start."

He read:

"My dear wife.

Don't be unhappy about the step I've taken. . . .

"Am about to take," she interrupted. "You couldn't have written it after you'd done it."

"I'm about to take, then." He crossed out the phrase and wrote above it.

"You'll have to write it again afterwards . . . it won't look right like that, full of alterations."

"Look, for Christ's sake, do you want to hear it or don't you?"

"Go on, then."

For a long time I've seen you slip away from me. Drink has become my only pleasure. I feel more and more isolated from life. I can't go on alone any longer, and the young girl I once loved no longer exists. Good-bye.

"What young girl?" she asked suspiciously.

"You, of course, damn it. Just you. Don't you even understand that."

44

She suddenly fell very quiet and looked down at the table. The young girl he once loved. . . .

"Oh, well," she said clearing her throat, "Oh yes."

She didn't know why she felt such an urge to cry. Surgical spirit, she said to herself. I must try to get hold of some surgical spirit at least, since he's mentioned alcohol. Afterwards I'll be free. Have the whole house to myself.

She sniffed back her tears and cleared her throat before she began to read :

"Darling,
I can't stand it any longer. We have drifted so far apart and I have nothing to live for but you. I'll leave you so that you can have some peace and I hope you'll be happier without me. If I thought you loved me, I wouldn't have to do this."

She stopped, feeling the tears on her cheeks; one of them fell on the paper and made a wet spot.

There was a long silence. He let his hand move up and down behind her back but at a slight distance from it. He never touched her.

"Well then . . . I suppose we can leave it at that," he said at last, and his voice sounded unusually rough.

She turned away from him and cried silently into her apron, her shoulders heaving.

"Why . . . why the hell are you crying?" he said irritably. "After all it was your idea. If you don't want to. . . ."

She straightened and wiped her face with the back of her hand.

"Give me the letter, then. No, you'll have to rewrite it first."

She sat down at the table, hiding her face in her arms; her back shuddered. He stood behind her, still uncertain, uneasy.

"Oh, come on now, listen." He gave her elbow a gentle push. "This is just for fun. It isn't at all serious. You don't want to kill me, I know that. It's just a game. Don't go on crying, for God's sake. Surely you know it was just for fun when I sneaked up behind you earlier. It was only to give you a fright. I never meant to hurt you. You understand that, don't you?"

She sobbed against the table.

"In any case," he said, "we might as well write these letters and hide them afterwards. And then if either of us is silly like this again we can say: 'You be careful, now' and then we can laugh at it all."

She raised her head and nodded.

"I suppose that's best. Then you won't be able to do stupid things again for I'll have your letter and you won't know what I might do to you in return."

He agreed eagerly.

"Exactly. It's all in fun. But just in case, you know, it won't do any harm to have these letters."

"You write yours again, then."

He did so and gave her the paper. She gave him hers.

They looked at each other solemnly. They almost felt they should shake hands.

"May I have my book back as well?"

"Of course," he said. "Of course. Or listen, let me read it first. Quite an interesting book, that. Would be nice to read it."

"All right then, if you insist." She wiped her face with her hands and gulped back the last of her tears.

46

"If you really are so interested in my hobby. I'm going to bed now in any case. Don't sit up too late."

He waved at her as she went, poured another glass of whisky and opened the book.

"Don't lie awake waiting for me, little woman. Sleep well. I'll be up soon."

10

SHE LAY tossing and turning in bed, unable to sleep.

'You go to bed, little woman. I'll be up soon; I just want to read a few pages first.' There was nothing threatening in that. And she couldn't have said that she wanted the book back immediately—not after the way things had been when they said good-night. It had almost seemed as if they had trusted one another, as though they liked one another again. She had thought it had been almost beautiful and hadn't wanted to start another quarrel. She regretted it now; now he was sitting down there reading the book and she blushed with shame as she thought about certain passages she had underlined or written herself.

What would he think? He would understand, surely he would. When she went to bed she had almost believed that he liked her, that it had been true when he said that it was all just a joke and that they might as well go the whole way and get the matter over and done with, and then be able to laugh about it. After that she had gone up to bed and he had stayed downstairs reading. But would he understand? She tried to picture the dangerous pages in her mind, tried to remember every detail and follow them word for word. One man had come home drunk in the middle of winter and his wife hadn't heard his knocking, or had pre-

48

tended not to, and the husband had frozen to death on the doorstep. It was in the country and nobody had known when he got home, or maybe somebody had heard him but didn't say so. In any case the wife was never suspected and the whole thing was put down as an accident.

But this was so very different. Surely he knew that that sort of thing could never happen to him. He was never that drunk and anyway he always drank at home; and if it did happen he could go and stay with the neighbours; and besides, it never got that cold.

But what she had written about the broken glass was worse. It was dangerous. And there was the note about someone who slipped on the soap in the bath and fell backwards, hit his head and drowned. And the wife who had accidentally knifed her husband—he had come and given her a hug just as she was cutting some meat and had a knife in her hand; the wife had been in despair and didn't even know how it had happened; it was manslaughter but everyone felt so sorry for the wife, as much as for the husband; it was never a question of murder—the poor woman was in a state of shock. She had underlined that bit!

She turned uneasily in bed, changed position, pulled the covers over her head, but still she couldn't sleep. She had almost been happy when they said good-night. She had not been afraid at all. She had not given a thought to killing him. Everything had been so much better than it had been for a long time. But now he was sitting down there reading the book. Perhaps he'd get angry again. . . . Perhaps he had felt like she had, that it was almost as though they liked each other again;

perhaps he too had felt happy and relieved, but then he had opened the book. . . .

She was sweating now, and tossing and turning all the time while the horror rose in her. *I must go down and have a look.* She felt an irresistible urge to find something to say: 'I couldn't sleep, so I thought I'd come down and sit here for a while. Have you found anything exciting?' 'I got so hungry that I had to have a sandwich . . .' 'It's late and you must get up tomorrow morning, you ought to go to bed soon!' Talk, just talk to make him put the book down, think of something to make him talk about something else. Just talking about anything would help. Only she was afraid that he would see through her and that it would make him hold on to the book even longer. *I'll get up anyway and have a look. I'll have a look through the door to see his expression; he needn't see me at all.*

She crept out of bed and fumbled bare-footed down the stairs. The kitchen door was slightly ajar, and holding her breath she poked her head through the opening and looked in. He was sitting in almost the same position as when she had left him, his head resting in his hands, his hair falling over his forehead, the whisky bottle half empty and a cigarette lying in a saucer. She drew a deep breath; *I've told him not to put his ash in the saucers. We've got enough ashtrays in this house for twenty people. It's me who has to . . .* But she let her breath out again, slowly in order to conceal her presence from him. No, she couldn't go in, she dared not.

He laughed a little to himself about something he had read, took another drink, turned the pages at random,

50

looked to see how many pages were left, took a puff of the cigarette and let it fall down on the table. *It'll make holes in the cloth. How often do I have to tell him that....* She stopped herself. He looked up from the book and she quickly withdrew her head from the door.

11

Ah ha, Ah ha! I see! So this is what the bitch fiddles with when I'm not here. I work my guts out from morning to night so that she can sit at home and have a nice time doing this. This!

He reached out for the glass without looking and drained it absent-mindedly. She was so cunning! Such a black soul she had. Talk about hobby! No woman would have such a morbid hobby without a reason. Murder after murder, and never any ordinary friendly murders, murders inspired by drink or sex—only murders committed in an unusual way and where the murderer got away with it. Wife murders husband. Husband murders wife. Unusual accidents. A wish to cry overwhelmed him and forced him to pour yet another glass of whisky. He had thought he had been wrong. There had been no cunning in his intentions, only honesty. He had sincerely regarded their letter-writing as a joke, and hoped that they could stop having horrible thoughts about killing each other. Honestly and sincerely he had walked up to her ready to shake hands, give her another chance. She had cried and sobbed—he had really felt sorry for her, almost wanted to give her a hug and caress her.

Poor old bag. After all, we used to like each other once. Now we must help each other to become friends again and get some sense into our relationship! That's

52

what he had thought, he had wanted to clear up every-thing between them, he had wondered whether he oughtn't to clean his shoes himself and help her clear the plates. He had believed in her. He had wanted to help her. He had thought she really was sorry about her lousy thoughts. And after all that she was so horrible, so ungrateful, so thoroughly deceitful.

He went on reading doggedly, and his anger still lurked inside him—it felt almost like sorrow. She must be rather frightened now, lying in bed knowing that he was about to find out everything about her. She knew that he had her letter, the letter she had written herself; he could sneak up and press a pillow over her face, just go on pressing till she stopped breathing and she could no longer scream, repay her justly for her deceit.

He thought he heard a sound by the door and raised his head, listening. Was the bitch standing behind the door watching him secretly? She was false all through, her sobbing had been a trick just to lure him into believing her, a typical woman's trick; perhaps she was standing outside at this very moment with a heavy vase in her hand, or the iron, just waiting for him to get up and leave the kitchen ... 'I'm going to bed now, come soon, don't sit up too late', she had said. But she hadn't gone up, it was lies, all of it; she was standing outside holding something heavy, with a sly expression on her face, and the letter in her hand, the letter in which he had written. . . .

He relaxed. The letter would be worthless if she killed him that way. With a broken skull he'd be a very strange suicide case. But what had she worked out now?

He looked round the room uneasily, observed every

object suspiciously. The tin-opener? The breadknife? Powdered glass in his food? Poison? Every familiar utensil became loaded with significance. So many accidents happen in kitchens, hadn't he read about that? The staircase—it could collapse. . . .

He sighed again, relieved. The staircase, yes. Who used it the most? Not him! He'd remember about the staircase. But she had the advantage of being at home all day—she could set a thousand traps and he would be defenceless when he came home in the evenings. . . .

Not tonight, though. She'll be prepared tonight. She'll be expecting mischief. I'll have to stay here all night, she won't be able to get at me here. I'll get up in a while when she's gone and lock the kitchen door, and sleep here on the floor, so she won't be able to do anything tonight. She can lie up there with all her plans! We shall see who is the cleverer of us!

12

AGAINST HER will she must have fallen asleep some time during the night for when she woke up she was lying in bed. It wasn't the alarm-clock that had woken her but the sunshine that had come licking in through the gap between the curtains. The alarm-clock had stopped. Neither of them had thought about winding it the previous night. She must have left her post by the kitchen door and gone up to bed some time during the night but she had only a faint recollection of it. She lay still, her head propped up on her arm, listening. The house was silent. She turned towards his bed and saw that it was empty, untouched; the pyjamas were still in their bag on top of the pillow.... Had he left already? Where had he gone? She got both legs out over the side of the bed but stayed there, her hands resting on her knees and her head hanging. She remembered everything that had happened, their quarrel, the book, the letters they had written.

Where was he? She started and looked behind her over her shoulder. Was he standing in the bathroom with a razor-blade in his hand, waiting for her? *Was he under the bed?* With a little shriek she pulled her feet up on to the bed again while she leaned over the edge of the bed to have a look underneath it. She almost expected to meet a pair of shiny, yellow eyes. But there was nothing except dust. With trembling hands she felt under her pillow for his letter. It was still there.

My dear wife,

Don't be unhappy because of the step I am about to take. For a long time I have seen you sliding away from me. Drink has become my only pleasure. I feel more and more isolated from life. I can't go on any longer alone, and the young girl I once loved no long exists. Good-bye.

She dressed quickly and stuck the letter inside her bra. That was one place he would never look for it, she thought bitterly. From now on she would always have to carry the letter with her. Not leave it anywhere. If she lost it, or he got it back from her, she would be helpless. Then she would only have to await her own suicide. She walked slowly up to the mirror and looked at herself, the wide-open eyes, the loosely hanging mouth. She tried to smile but only a grimace of horror showed in the mirror. She brushed her hair and then stood blinking and pulling her facial muscles to make them softer, tried to bring them under control to be able to smile more naturally. He had to be somewhere. She would have to meet him somewhere.

What if he had already left home? But where would he go? No, he wouldn't have gone; he might have thought of it to get away from her and what he suspected her of planning, but he would have to stay here if he were to get hold of her. Perhaps he was waiting for her outside the gate with the car? But then he wouldn't be able to make use of the letter. Yes, if he said she had thrown herself in front of the car and that he hadn't seen her till it was too late. But when they took her to

56

the hospital injured, they would find his letter inside
her bra. . . .

She had to laugh. It really was a good idea. She
would survive and he would be accused of attempted
murder. But then if he showed them her letter? She
shook her head to get her thoughts sorted out. It was
too difficult, too complicated, she'd never manage it.
She wished she could ask him to change the letters
back, forget about the whole business, go on as before.
At least it would be better than this. Or perhaps they
could give a little more thought to the possibility of a
divorce. Or perhaps even. . . . When they had said good
night. . . .

13

SHE STOPPED at the top of the stairs. It's possible to fix a string across the stairs so that the person who walks down them. . . . She bent down to feel with her hand but there was nothing. And mind the letter. . . . She shook her head several times, had to stop thinking like this. She had to get it out of her head. It really was too silly! Everything was just the same. Everything was the same as before. She would cook a nice dinner tonight, they would laugh together and tear up the letters.

The kitchen door was still ajar and she peered in. The light was on and he was sitting at the table as he had been the night before, his head resting between his out-stretched arms. The book lay under his head. She glanced at the kitchen clock. They never used to be up so early. Half past six. She stood, undecided, wondering whether she should go back upstairs to sleep. But that would only be postponing the inevitable; she would lie there turning in her bed, unable to sleep, only waiting for the moment when she had to look him in the eyes and talk to him.

She crept forward silently. If he had left her letter lying about. . . . She'd be able to take it back. Burn it! Hide it! She noticed the whisky bottle was empty. If she was lucky he might have forgotten about the letters when he woke up. 'What letter are you talking about? You must have been dreaming. There you are, drunk as usual, sitting at the kitchen table asleep, and you don't care that I lie awake worrying; look how you've messed up the tablecloth, ash everywhere, you know we've got millions of ashtrays!'

Her hand went to her bra where the letter was hidden. If she could make him believe that he had dreamed it all then she wouldn't have to. . . . And she would still have his. Nice to think about when he got nasty and scolded her or ordered her about, complained about the food, or made remarks about her housekeeping. Then he'd be sorry! He would bulldoze over her like the great bully he was, not realising that she had a weapon to free herself of him, so easily, so safely. . . .

She smiled to herself and sneaked forward to get a better look at him. He was snoring and breathing heavily. His face was red, his hands looked dirty. She felt loath to touch him. If he'd only go on sleeping. If only he were dead already. No, he was breathing. How perfect it would have been otherwise. He had died during the night. The letter was found by his side in the morning. She began to cry and rushed over to him. She'd have to get her letter back, so they wouldn't find it on him. Afterwards she'd . . . acetone, chloroform.

No, she had only a little carbon tetrachloride. Carbon tetrachloride and paint thinners. Children could die from breathing large doses of thinners. What if she opened the bottle and put it under his nose. . . . She began to tremble with excitement. It was the only way. The only safe way. He could have done that himself. He was drunk and didn't take any notice of what was in the bottle he took out . . . perhaps he had even drunk some of it . . . or he fell asleep with it under his nose. She sneaked past him on trembling legs and reached up to the cupboard. He muttered something in his sleep, his head fell down from the arm it had been resting on. She stopped still, not a muscle moved in her face, her eyes were wide open. No . . . go on sleeping!

A deep snort rose from his throat, followed by a cackling gasp which revealed blackened, badly cared-for teeth. He lifted his head from the table, shook it and gasped again.

"Wha's sa time?" he mumbled.

She gave a start.

"Oh, the time? Half past six. Twenty to seven."

"Why the hell didn't you wake me up?"

"Because we never usually get up at half past six. How was I to know where you were anyway? Have you been sitting here drinking all night? If you knew how I've been. . . ."

"You could at least have woken me and told me to go to bed!" he roared, and hammered his fist on the table. "What the hell is the matter with you? Couldn't you have made sure I got to bed?"

"I see, so that's how it is. You get drunk in the evenings and now *I'm* supposed to carry you to bed, huh?"

He blinked and stretched his arms, then he became aware of the open book on the table. He gave a quick laugh and patted his chest.

"Yes, indeed. That's how it is!"

"What do you mean?"

"I've been reading some interesting literature, last night. Very interesting." He gave the book a push so that it fell off the table on to the floor, its pages flapping.

Quicker than her thoughts she jumped up and picked

it up off the floor. She turned towards him, the book pressed tightly against her bosom.

"Now you've read it can I have it back?"

He got up slowly.

"Certainly. Of course you can. You just keep it."

He stalked across to the door and said over his shoulder:

"See that you get some coffee going while I go upstairs and dress."

14

HE RINSED his face and hands in icy water, brushed his teeth and shaved. He felt rather uplifted today. Things were out in the open. Now he knew. Everything fitted. She could keep her bloody book. She wouldn't or couldn't use any of those tricks she had put in it anyway. He was on his guard. He whistled while he finished shaving. Cowardly and pitiful, ugly and afraid, that was what she was. Sitting there fiddling with her bits of paper and her writings. When it came to it she wouldn't really dare, after all. She was too much of a coward, too soft. She had cried herself to death that time when she had pushed him out of the window. Cried so the tears had flowed in rivers, and hugged him and kissed him till he felt like being sick; unable to move in his plaster cast he hadn't been able to avoid her silly messing about. Saying how she loved him, how afraid she was of losing him, so sorry she was about the accident, how she blamed herself. Probably she was pottering about in the kitchen now. Bitter and sour. She had hidden the book already, of course. Childishness! Perhaps thinking of adding a little something extra to the coffee? Her and her poisons, no, she wouldn't dare.

He went over to the medicine cupboard to have a look. Elastoplast, Tampax—did she really still need those?—old lipsticks and hairpins, eye-wash, cotton wool, aspirins—he frowned when he saw the aspirins but went past them—cough mixture, pills for diarrhoea and for constipation, iron tablets, gargle which she never used, her old dead father's heart tablets—he paused—gentian violet; he didn't know much about that.

Really he ought to take the day off from work and go to the library to have a look at some medical books. No, chemistry books. He ought to go to the doctor as well and say that he couldn't sleep, ask for some sleeping tablets. It would be even more cunning to go to several doctors and get a whole lot of them. Strange that she didn't have any sleeping tablets, surely women her age normally did. They were at home all day and had nothing better to do but to think about how ill they were, how they couldn't sleep at night and how painful their backs or heads or stomachs were. Of course, she might have a secret supply somewhere. Perhaps in the kitchen. He'd have to get her out of the house one day so he could have a good look around. In the meantime he would remove the heart medicine.

He began to tie his shoes, chuckling. Combing his hair, he was careful to conceal the small bald patch at the crown of his head. He suddenly felt high-spirited, with no hint of a hangover. His head was as steady and strong as his hands. He selected a tie, knotted it meticulously and straightened his jacket, studying himself in the mirror. Everything had fallen into place. Now he knew where he had her. Her whimpering, cowardice and slyness, he would make her swallow it all. He would irritate her a little, scorn her, sneak in on her often, like he had done last night, put bait out for her—he laughed noisily—push her on the stairs; scare the wits out of her while he decided how he'd eventually get rid of her.

15

WHEN HE came down the table was laid nicely, the remains of his overnight stay in the kitchen had been removed; there was coffee and fresh bread on the table and several kinds of cheese and jam.

"Good morning, little wife," he said and patted her behind as he walked past her. She gave a start and looked sourly at him over her shoulder.

"What makes you so cheerful?"

"Why shouldn't I be?" he asked in a friendly voice and sat down.

"No poison in the coffee, I hope?"

She glared at him.

They ate for a while in silence.

"Good coffee this. Really good coffee this."

"Glad you like it. Though it's the same coffee you have every morning."

"Listen," she went on after having looked at the tablecloth for a while and stirred her coffee far longer than necessary.

"Yes?"

"Well, about what happened yesterday."

"Yesterday? What happened yesterday?"

How could she say anything when he went on like this? How could she manage? Perhaps he *had* taken it all seriously? Perhaps he had prepared some nasty trap for her upstairs, perhaps that was why he was in such a

64

good mood. And she had wasted all her chances by nagging him again; she ought to have been cheerful instead and played up to him; perhaps then she might have persuaded him. . . .

"I've got such an incredibly strange letter you've written me," she said finally and looked him straight in the eyes.

"Have you started reading my old love letters?" he asked and started to chuckle.

"You know what I mean."

"Not really," he said lightly and stretched out for the sugar bowl.

Had she dreamt it all? Her head felt so heavy and strange; he wasn't himself and she was no longer sure what was dream and what was reality.

"Oh, don't sit there being funny," she said. "You know very well what we did last night."

He looked at her with narrow eyes.

"You know, about committing suicide."

"Yes?"

"Well, I think it's all childish. I'm not thinking of committing suicide and surely you aren't either."

"No, you can be sure of that," he said with a laugh.

Why did he sound so self-assured? Did he have a plan already? She fumbled with her dressing gown by her bosom but snatched her hand away when she felt that he was observing her closely.

I want my letter back! She didn't voice the words, but the cry echoed in her head, hammered against her skull.

"Look after yourself while I'm away, little woman," he said amiably as he got up.

"Are you going already? You don't usually go to

work so early." She couldn't conceal her uneasiness as she ran up to him and held him by the arm; he mustn't go till they'd discussed it; she wouldn't dare do it tonight, she wouldn't be able to make him talk about it tonight and it would be too late.

He pulled himself loose of her grasp and slapped the hand which was reaching out for him.

"Yes, I've got to go now. I want to have a look at some things, want to think about various things."

She stood in the doorway eyeing him uneasily and twisting her fingers.

"Couldn't you stay a little longer—surely it can't be that important. . . ."

He pushed her aside roughly.

"I don't know what you're gabbling about, woman," he said. "Take a few aspirins and lie down till your head clears. *Take a lot of aspirins!*" he laughed loudly.

Then he picked up his hat and walked out through the front door.

16

HE HAD a plan; she knew for certain now that he had a plan. Oh, why had she spoilt her chances. Now she'd never get hold of that letter of hers. Naturally, he had it with him when he left. He would go out now and get hold of something to kill her with. Her hands were shaking as she pulled the kitchen curtain and saw him driving out of the garage. He raised his hand and waved to her. He was so sure of himself! She let go of the curtain and stood clenching her fists in mounting terror. Dear, dear God. Forgive me my sins. What if I go to church and talk to the priest. No. He might think that I...! He might think I've gone mad! I can't talk to anybody!

She rushed upstairs. Aspirins! Why had he mentioned aspirins? Had he done something to them? She found the bottle and with trembling hands poured them all down the toilet and pulled the chain. She could clearly see he had been fiddling about in the medicine cupboard, everything that had been moved and he had put nothing back in its place. Had he taken anything? She couldn't remember everything that had been there before. Her head was spinning. She'd have to go and buy something to calm her nerves, something that would make her sleep.

What was his plan? Was it something he had got from the book? She would have to read it from beginning to end and try to find out what could have appealed to him. She must calm down. Be cool. He had thought of something and she'd have to anticipate it, and get her letter back. Or think of something herself. Something that wasn't noted down in her book, something he would never dream of. After all, she had his letter. If she could fix him before he did anything to her, then she would be the survivor, the house would be hers, everything would be hers; he would be out of the way and she would be free; he would have committed suicide. Her eyes hardened. She mustn't get frightened. She must take it very easily and think coolly and clearly. She had the upper hand, she was at home in the house all day. She had innumerable hours to herself and her plans, to do all the preliminary work.

As long as he didn't come home early. She didn't know where he had gone. . . . Perhaps he had just gone to fetch something and would be back soon! She didn't know how much time she had left to think, to plan. She mustn't waste any of it.

She went back into the kitchen and locked the door behind her. She had the book with her and she now sat down, opened it and began to read. He wouldn't be able to sneak in on her this time. If he came he wouldn't be able to open the door. She would read and try to follow his train of thoughts from the night before, try to see what his mind had taken a liking to. He wasn't particularly cunning, so probably it would be something quite unsophisticated. She was the cunning one. She would be prepared when he returned and at the same time she would have to make plans for a counter-attack.

68

17

DAMN IT! What a bitch! Damn her! What has she
done? I still can't believe it. No, I can't believe it. It
isn't like her. Of course she's sour and peevish and
horrible but I really didn't think . . . I didn't think she
was *that* bad. Of course, she isn't the same person as she
was then, a long time ago. . . . She, who was beautiful
and loving and never wanted to leave me, nothing was
too good for me . . . no. Of course, one can't expect
that sort of thing to last for ever. Damned stupid! As
I told her many times: 'Life isn't like that, life is more
serious than that, one has to take a hold of oneself,
stop being soft.' But at any rate, one did think she'd be
loyal, at least, that all her promises meant something.

No, she had always been like she was now, only he
hadn't seen it. He felt the sweat of sudden realisation
glueing the hairs to his forehead. She probably hadn't
meant a word of what she'd said. Just behaved like that
to soften him. It was the house she had wanted all the
time, a nice house to live in and money in the bank, that
was what it was. She hadn't cared a damn for him. But
no doubt he had been the dumbest, the most guileless
bloke she could lay her hands on. Nobody else would
have been so bloody stupid as to take her. What an
idiot he was. How bloody stupid. To have let himself
be cheated and not even found out. . . . It's enough to
make one cry. . . . Everything he had fought for, all

that he had worked for, a peaceful old age, kindness and sympathy, all in vain. All of it.

He took a small bottle out of his trousers pocket and studied it for a long while, turning the bottle in his hand. His father-in-law's heart medicine. Why had it been kept in the medicine cupboard for so long? How much had been in it when the old man left? Had the contents slowly disappeared? What had really happened that time a few months ago when he had felt peculiar, when he sweated a lot and his heart had played up . . . he remembered now how she had bent over him looking worried, yet she'd been bloody happy inside, hadn't she? 'You'll soon be better', she had said and stroked his forehead. And smiled at him. Judas, Judas.

Why hadn't the medicine been thrown away? The old man had, after all, stayed with them only a few weeks while his own cow was in hospital with a broken leg. It had been hell having the old fellow there, for he was senile and quarrelsome and difficult to handle. Of course, she had taken her father's side all the time, and he had had to sit between them. As it happened the old man hadn't lived for long. But why was his medicine still there? The bottle ought to have been thrown away when he died. But *he* had it now; the key to the problem, maybe. He ought to find out what the ingredients were. Go somewhere and have the contents analysed, and also remember to ask what the symptoms would be if one took it without having heart trouble. . . . He would get a new nail for the bitch's coffin. Traitress. Traitress.

Where could he go? How could he find out about it? He considered the bottle, unscrewed the lid, smelled it. Put his little finger to the opening and turned it upside down, tasted the brownish grains that had settled on the tip of his finger. It tasted of hardly anything, a trifle bitter, a kind of flat taste. But poisonous?

There were better poisons. Rat poison. Weed-killer—all kinds of rubbish that killed insects and parasites. She would get what she deserved.

18

SHE WAS standing in the bedroom, pulling and shoving. I must move this bed somehow! I must be mad, daring to lie here all last night when he could have come in at any time and got into bed next to me and . . . and . . . strangled me, suffocated me, taken hold of me! If he came anywhere near me up here now I would scream. He wants to kill me! And here I am alone, a poor, lonely, defenceless woman. . . . I can't move the bed out of here. It won't go through the door. But, for God's sake, it must have come in some time, since it wasn't let down through the roof. . . . I'll never manage to turn it over and get it out on my own and . . . I can't do it. . . . It might fall down the stairs and end up in the corner there. That won't do. It needs two to hold it and shift it, one at each end. Where can I go? Where? I can't sleep on the floor. I'll have to go somewhere. *He* ought to move out of the room and sleep somewhere else; he started it all. It's my room and I have a right to sleep where I want in my own house. No, he'll never agree to that, he might start shouting and bawling, and what if he hits me. No, I'll have to make the sacrifice, as usual. Well in a way it's much better, much more practical, much safer for me to have him in here. Then he'll know where I've got him, and I'll be able to sneak in here in the night without having to turn the light on. . . .

She tore the bedclothes off her own bed and carried them across to the room opposite. It was her sewing room, or rather the lumber-room for it was a long time since she had last bothered to sew anything. He didn't notice what she wore anyway. It smelt slightly stuffy as nobody had been in there for a long time. The windows were closed and had been since her last big spring-cleaning—when was it, now? Not since before she had polished the windows anyway—she had only gone in there when she had to, when something was to be put away there or she had to find something. She put the mattress in a corner after she had pushed away some old magazines, some old shoes, a folded up mat, clothes that needed mending, socks to be darned—the smell lingered in her nose, washing his socks wasn't enough, they stank just the same, impregnated with his heavy, sour foot-sweat. Old letters, postcards, curtain rails...she kicked at the mess, shovelled it out of the way and then put down the mattress and made her bed on the floor.

When that was done she felt tired and sat down on the mattress. Piles all around her, piles of rubbish . . . rusty nails in a tin. There was a small toolbox there too; that was the one he used when he did something in the house, which was seldom. But he had insisted on having a toolbox and it was still there. The key was in it, it wouldn't be difficult to open. Aha! Perhaps it was a bit of good luck that she had come in here first. A small saw. She ran it across her arm, and it left a small white mark. She might as well take her own life, get out of all this, not have to struggle and toil, work like a slave just to keep herself alive, and to try to avoid all his foul rebukes, his swearing, his brutality. She might as well do it. Saw herself to death. Lie down in the bath and just let the

73

blood run. Oh, she almost wished she had the courage.

What did it matter if he escaped the blame, she could write a new letter herself, a true one; he might die of shock when he came home and found her lying there. . . . Never, never would he get over it, he would never forgive himself, never. He would remember how good she had been to him and how much fun they had had together—until he started. . . . That would be his punishment . . . the real punishment—realising that she wasn't as sly, as horrible as he had tried to make out she was. There he would be, with all his plans, unable to carry out any of them. He would be frustrated, wish that he had her back. . . . She might as well do it. It was just as good as this. But, wouldn't it make it too easy for him? Wouldn't she in death have complied with his wishes? No, better to hit herself with a hammer, suffocate herself, make it look as though he had done it! That would be justice. She would die, she didn't want to live when things were like this anyway, when all that she had tried to do was just trampled under his feet, but he would experience much more than a bad conscience when she was gone; he would get his just deserts.

He had no more right to the house and the money than she; no, he wasn't going to get it all and sit there afterwards having a good time, perhaps rejoicing that he had got rid of her, perhaps have other women there. . . . He should lose it all and go to jail, that was the only just way. Then he could feel sorry for himself. Being in jail was even worse than being dead. Guilty, guilty, because he had spoilt her life, made her what she was now, made her life so empty and meaningless that she might as well die. . . .

74

She sat on the mattress a little longer, taking the tools in her hands one by one, looking at them, testing them carefully against her skin. She would have to hide the saw somewhere so he couldn't find it and turn it against her before she had used it on herself. She put it by the head of her bed and draped a few pieces of cloth over it to conceal it from him if he should come into the room.

Then she got up, left the room and walked downstairs. She had pen and paper in her desk, where she had sat reading and writing in her little book—so long ago. How touching it seemed now, her sitting there cutting and glueing, ignorant of what would happen when he found the book and soiled it with his thoughts—but now all that had come to an end. It had been part of a game, something that had brought a little excitement and vitality into her thoughts. But now it was for real, it was a matter of life and death. She took out pen and paper and wrote:

Dear Mum,

It's a long time since I last wrote but nothing good has happened here and I know how it always upsets you to hear my bad news. That's why I haven't written to you for some time. But I suppose you'll have to hear from me sooner or later—before it gets too late. Yes, he's the same as ever, which you will probably understand. You know what a burden I have to bear. I wish I had listened to you when you warned me long ago.

But I was young and in love, I couldn't see his faults and had to go my own way. Well, it's too late now for regrets, what's done is done and you know I've had my punishment. Lately it has been worse than usual. I don't know what has come over him this time but he is drinking more than ever before, and hardly an evening goes by without him getting at the whisky. It's me who has to take care of everything, but I suppose one ought to be grateful as long as one doesn't have to wipe up sick.

Oh, if only you knew what I'm going through. He's become introspective, bad-tempered and the only time he talks to me is when he finds fault with me and quarrels. Nothing is right for him any more everything I do is wrong. This morning he hit me when I tried to kiss him goodbye. I really do wish everything could be as it was before. It is obvious that he isn't well but you know how impossible it is to get him to go to a doctor. Well, I suppose I'll just have to hope for the best. If only he wouldn't look at me as strangely as he does sometimes. I'm almost afraid that he might try to harm me.

Well, you know how it is. Everything is all right otherwise. The weather has been very nice lately although it has been raining a little. Thank goodness Dad left us in time and didn't have to see me like this. But I hope you'll live to see the day when everything is right again, and I hope you can come and stay with me soon.

She read through the letter, thought for a while and then added :

Couldn't you try and come as soon as possible? I would feel much safer here if I didn't have to be alone in the house with him.

Much love and many kisses.

19

"THANK YOU, thank you, that's very kind of you," he said, forcing a laugh. "I must say how glad I am you had time to see me, Doctor. One doesn't like to come and be a trouble like this, but. . . ."

"That's all right," said the doctor in a tired voice. "It isn't all that much trouble. Perhaps if you wouldn't mind telling . . ." he glanced at his watch—"I have surgery from three o'clock, you see I'm only really supposed to deal with industrial cases full-time. You know, these days!" he added with a sigh.

"Of course, I understand. You see, the thing is this— well, maybe you'll think it's nothing, Doctor, nothing serious in a big strong man; but you see one needs one's sleep, especially when the job is as tiring as mine."

The doctor looked as though he was listening. He raised his head as soon as there was a silence.

"Yes?"

"Well, you see, it's about my sleep. I don't suppose I'm the first one—whatever the reason . . . with a hard job like mine it isn't surprising that I'm tired when I come home in the evenings, of course, but one way and another I never feel as though I get any proper rest; you know how it is, Doctor, you lie there tossing and turning and can't fall asleep, and just when you're about to doze off someone slams a car door and then everything is lost—you understand, I'm sure, Doctor . . ."

He shifted uneasily on the chair, felt his breathing was irregular and forced, hoped that that would help his sick-man image. The doctor didn't seem to notice. If only he knew how he had sounded. Normal, naturally, absolutely normal. The doctor couldn't even be bothered to listen. People came and queued here to tell the doctor that they couldn't sleep, he was no different from anybody else. It *was* true, of course. Nearly true, anyway. He used to lie awake for a long time before he could fall asleep. He never fell asleep before she did, and sometimes he would wake up in the middle of the night, and lie there listening to her snores and mumbling. They talk about men being the ones who snore, but they should hear her!

He really did find it difficult to sleep. And anyway, nearly everybody took sleeping tablets these days. They were in every home. It was quite common. He really couldn't sleep and he'd get the tablets and it would just be a terrible accident that the wife had been feeling bad for some time; she had seen the tablets and taken some—too many. Surely it wasn't his fault? Of course, she had been depressed, and of course he had noticed and tried to help her as best he could, talked to her, asked her to confide in him. But no, she wouldn't tell him anything. Would sooner carry on alone, feeling ill, and God only knows what she was thinking about. How was he to know? He hadn't imagined that it was that serious. After all, she hadn't said anything. If only he had had the faintest idea. . . . Now he blamed himself, he should of course have hidden the tablets, but he just didn't have any idea that she would do such a thing. . . .

He smiled uneasily.

"Well, probably you think this all sounds very silly, Doctor. A strong man like me shouldn't come here complaining about this sort of thing. I've tried taking hot milk too, but it didn't help. And you know how it is, Doctor, when one has to get up in the mornings and go to work; it's often difficult."

The doctor played with his pen and gave him a friendly look.

"Have you suffered for long?"

"From what?"

"Well, insomnia, of course. What you are suffering from now."

"Well, that. Yes. No, not so terribly long. Perhaps a fortnight, a month or so. I can't say for certain when it started, I mean, it kind of sneaks up on you, it isn't easy to tell. Only when you've been awake night after night like that for a while, well, it gets difficult to cope with things and you think it might be better if you got something to give you a proper night's rest."

He gestured deprecatingly.

"I know it sounds womanish. But I thought I'd come just the same and have a word with you, Doctor, since ... you were here, and ask if. . . ."

"Yes, yes," said the doctor absent-mindedly. "You can't go round like that of course. Naturally you need your sleep at night. Do you feel all right otherwise?"

Well now, did he? He couldn't keep track of all his thoughts. Was he perhaps a little seedy—ought he to be? 'No, thank you, I'm all right but my wife . . . she's worse. Well, I have felt a little strange lately, unsettled in a way; I don't feel like doing anything, could it be my nerves, doctor?' That was no good either. Perhaps the doctor would remember later on if anything happened, that he had had something wrong with his nerves.

"Well, yes. I'm not as young as I was and it's beginning to show in my back, but otherwise there's nothing much wrong with me." He laughed as best he could.

"No headaches, stomach trouble, tiredness during the day?"

"No. Well, naturally I'm tired. But that's only because I don't get any sleep at night."

The doctor yawned. He wrote out a prescription and handed it over.

20

THE DOORBELL rang.

She was still sitting by her desk. She froze to a rigid stillness, her tongue arrested in the act of licking the stamp. Who was it? Who? Was it him? Had he come back? Was it something dangerous? Who wanted to see her?

It was half past three. He oughtn't to be back for another two hours. Was it him?

It rang again and somebody was knocking too. Important? Urgent? Who? Why? She hadn't spoken to anyone, not asked anyone to come. Nobody ever came. Perhaps there was something called telepathy and her mother had seen her writing and read the letter, had had some kind of supernatural message that her daughter was in danger—but she couldn't have got there *that* quickly. It was always the same, nobody ever called. The woman next door came sometimes to borrow a cup of flour, but never at this time of day. Nobody ever came this time of day . . . not even the post.

It might be some salesman. Or some of those young boys and girls who sometimes came and wanted to talk to her about God. That would be nice, she usually felt quite uplifted after they had been, it was so wonderful to meet these devout young people. After she had married she had, more or less, had to give up her religion. It was impossible to get him to church and it wasn't the same going alone. If anyone needed to go to church it was him, but he was too stubborn. It could be some of those young people so she might as well open the door. Or even if it was just a salesman. It certainly wouldn't be a friend who had come for a chat. People knew about his bad temper and how it ruined her nerves; she didn't have many friends—that's what happens when you have problems, people avoid you— she had better go to the door. Suppose it was the police? Could he have gone to the police and told them about her? You could never be sure with him. She wouldn't put it past him. He would do anything to embarrass her.

She got up quietly and walked up to the window by the stairs, which overlooked the front door. A man in uniform. It was true! She would never open it, they'd have to break in the door. But at least it wasn't a police uniform. And so what, even if it had been, what had she done wrong? She hadn't done anything they could punish her for. If he had talked to the police he would be worse off than her. She would tell them what he had done and then he would find out who'd be worse off.

She reached the door just as the bell rang for the third time, and opened it so quickly that she nearly fell out on to the porch. This policeman or whoever he was shouldn't get away until he had heard what she had to say, she had to tell them, then maybe she would have a chance to have him taken care of and she could feel safe in the house again. . . . But it wasn't the police. A young man, telegram, he said, and then he was gone after a quick searching look at her.

Telegram! Telegram? Surely mother couldn't have . . . she tore it open with trembling hands.

WE KNOW EVERYTHING ABOUT YOU. BE
CAREFUL OR WE'LL REVEAL EVERYTHING.
AWAIT FURTHER INSTRUCTIONS.

Her heart was hammering so it showed even through
her clothes. She could feel cold sweat on her face and
under her arms. She folded the telegram and hid it in
her stocking, looking all around her as though she
expected him to be standing behind her even now,
having read it over her shoulder. It hadn't been signed.
Her eyes were wide open and a tear fell on her cheek.
It was him! It had to be. He was trying to frighten her!
He sat at his desk and sent the telegram on his firm's
telephone, laughing to himself at her horror, thought
he could make her powerless. It must be from him. Who
else could it be? Who? Nobody, nobody could know.
She hadn't seen a soul since she went out shopping this
morning, even less let anyone know. . . .

What if he hadn't done it. What if he'd been telling
tales? He might have told his workmates. That would
be so like him. That was just the kind of thing he would
do, no sense of loyalty at all. He would describe what
they had done, what he had said, how he had
frightened her and pretended to try and strangle her,
talk about her scrap-book. Tell his version of the story,
make her out to be some kind of witch. And later his
mates would sit there thinking about how horrible she
was, that she had really started it all, believe his lies and
fantasies and then try to make money out of the business.
'Await further instructions!' Blackmail! Oh, he had
surprised her. He had outwitted her. Hadn't she been
here all day, only thinking about protecting herself,
even considered taking her own life for his sake, and all

the time he had been laughing and telling it all as a fine story, God knows to whom, God knows to how many people, perhaps the whole firm were now laughing at the fool of a wife he had, the poor man.

No, no, if they wanted money she would never be able to pay. How could she? She had nothing to pay with. He had his hands on all the cash; her housekeeping money hardly covered the cost of the food—and for all that he complained that she was wasting it. Never a penny did she have left to herself. She stood in the middle of the floor, sweating, her hair sticking clammily to her scalp. Something had to be done immediately. Something that would stop all this once and for all, no matter which way, just so long as it stopped. She put on her coat and ran down to the letter-box.

21

"HUBBIE'S HERE! Are you at home?"

He didn't think himself that his voice sounded natural. He didn't normally shout like that. She would tell him off and nag him because he shouted and didn't wipe his feet when he came in. But as he had walked up to the house he had suddenly had a strange feeling of something ominous awaiting him. The house seemed dead behind its closed, dirty windows; no lights were on and it was absolutely quiet. Would she be standing behind the front door with something in her hand? He had felt a sudden urge to be noisy and make a fuss just to show that he wasn't afraid. This was a normal household; isn't it normal for husbands to call out like that when they come home to their nice castle after the day's toil and sweat?

So, there he was. At his usual time. Not that he was a bit ashamed or took the slightest notice of her—no, he just came in, making a lot of noise. That was just like him, to laugh and try to pretend that nothing had happened, as though he always made so much noise. He must be up to something, otherwise he would have been like he normally was—he must have something up his sleeve, something he would do to her. I'll pretend not to notice, pretend that nothing has happened. I won't let him think that I've seen through him. I'm ready for him.

"Oh, so there you are. I didn't expect to see you here again after the way you left this morning, without even saying goodbye."

"Surely you couldn't have got it into your head that I'd thought of leaving home. My own home?" He laughed noisily and walked up to her and patted her back.

She stepped backwards.

"Don't you dare touch me like that. Take off your shoes when you come in and put on some slippers. It's bad enough that you come in yourself—you needn't bring in a load of dirt as well."

Distance. Keep him at a distance. I mustn't let him get near me.

"Happy and charming as usual," he said scornfully. "And how have you spent your day, then?"

"I? What do I do every day? I think it's me who should ask you that question. . . . It's you who gets out and meets people, you should have something to talk about. But since you are so interested, I can tell you that I have rearranged the furniture."

"Surely not a new put-u-up, I hope?" he asked and took a step towards her. "Those you read about that collapse during the night suffocating the sleeper?"

"No, but I would have got one if I'd had the money," she answered, annoyed. "I tell you, I don't intend to sleep in the same room as you after what's happened. I ought to have moved out years ago. Then perhaps I might have been a little happier in my own home. But from now on I'm going to sleep in the sewing room."

"The lumber-room, you mean. That'll suit you fine."

She wanted to burst into tears. She wanted to say: 'Do you remember when we moved in . . .' but instead she said:

86

"Well, that's how it's going to be. You ought to be happy that I didn't take your filthy sheets in there and let you sleep on the floor instead. But then we know how you would have complained. No, *I'm* sleeping on the floor."

He controlled an impulse to run upstairs immediately to see what alterations she had made up there. Perhaps that was just what she wanted him to do. It could all be a lie, her having moved things about, perhaps she had quite a different surprise waiting for him. He'd have to get up there to check before he went to bed so that he wasn't unprepared when he went in there later.

"Is supper ready?"

"I haven't touched it yet. I know you don't trust me so I thought it would be better to wait till you were back," she grinned at him.

"Indeed! Well, if you really want me to stand behind you and check everything you do, I shan't mind. It's probably the only way to make you do anything in this house anyway."

"I wrote to my mother today," she said in an off-hand tone.

"So the old cow is still alive?"

"Oh yes, she is. And I hope she will live for a long time. I've asked her to come here."

"You've asked her to come here? To my house?"

He grabbed hold of her and started to shake her.

"Surely that's up to me. She's my mother. The way you're behaving I could do with having someone in the house; I never know what you're up to the way you're carrying on. . . ."

She suddenly began to cry. It just came, unexpectedly. She hadn't wanted to. She ought not let him see her

87

crying. She didn't want him to know how much he had hurt her; that would only make him feel bigger and more self-assured.

He stood holding her by the shoulders, flabbergasted. This! The old bitch staying in the house! Perhaps they would never get rid of her—she was old, God knows how long she might stay for. And they would be two against him. Not just *one* awful bitch to fight, but two . . . two who worked together. He knew that her mother had never wanted them to get married, she had been against it all the time. If only she had had her way, then. If only she had objected a little more strongly and got it all cancelled. He didn't stand a chance with both of them in the house, he wouldn't dare go out for fear of what they might conjure up while he was away, and he wouldn't be able to stay at home with them all day. Nattering, gossiping, nagging, scheming and perhaps even worse. If she told her mother what had happened and made the old woman believe that she was in some kind of danger. . . .

"You can't be serious," he said helplessly. "It isn't fair. You're not giving me a chance. Don't fetch her over here, for God's sake. . . ."

"And why not, if you don't mind me asking? Are you afraid of having her in the house, maybe? Is it because she might stop you doing something you had thought about. Do you think I don't know the reason?"

No. No. He'd have to prevent it. He'd have to do something. Not to be able to live in one's own house any more, something had to happen, he'd have to get rid of her, anything, before this happened.

"What did you write to her?"

"What do you think? What could I write? I was

88

forced to ask her to come and stay here because I'm afraid of what you might do to me."

"Did you tell her . . . ?"

"No. I didn't tell her what you tried to do to me yesterday. I'm not that mean. I'm not like certain others who babble to everybody about their private affairs. I'm not the sort of person who opens his mouth without first thinking who's listening."

"And what's that supposed to mean?" he asked and looked at her intently.

She turned her face away. Tried to disappear inside herself, pretend that he didn't exist. She wished she hadn't mentioned the letter to her mother. It had just slipped out, she had never intended to talk about it. It was idiotic of her to have said anything. Now he'd do anything to stop her, perhaps he would. . . . And what if he hadn't said anything to anyone, if he hadn't said anything to his mates. Well, in that case, the telegram must have been from him and he was amused now because it had frightened her.

Should I tell him I've received a telegram? He'll only laugh. He'll say he doesn't know anything about it. I'm not supposed to know he sent it. He thinks he's frightened me. Well, he's succeeded. Now it's his turn to be frightened.

"You can let go of me now," she said. "You know it'll be a couple of days before Mum arrives. We can discuss it later."

22

THEY HAD eaten in silence. She cleared away and washed up while he sat by the table.

"Listen," he said.

"Yes?"

"I was thinking a little at work today."

"Well?"

"I mean, I've come to the conclusion that we're probably run down, both of us. I mean, we used to be able to get along together before. Now—like it's been the last few days, it shouldn't be necessary for us to be like that all the time."

She held her breath.

"So I thought, why don't I try to get a little holiday and we could go away for a few days. It would be so nice to get away for a couple of days for a change. Breathe a bit of fresh air and see something new and then...."

"Are you really serious?" she asked feebly.

"Yes, God damn it. We can't go on like this much longer, for Christ's sake. I.... It was silly of me to sneak in on you like I did yesterday. But I was only joking. You know that, don't you?"

Tears came to her eyes again and she walked over to him.

"It isn't just something you're saying—about a holiday—so that I don't fetch Mum here."

"No, damn it. Why must you always take everything that way? Couldn't you believe what I say for once?"

"It isn't easy to tell . . ." she answered tonelessly.

"No, but now I'm saying it at any rate. We've got stuck in routine and humdrum, both of us. We've got irritable and all that. What do you say?"

"Where should we go, if you took a holiday?"

"Well, I haven't thought about that yet. I was just toying with the idea, you know. If things could only be like they used to be. At least we could try again."

Something softened in her, she didn't know what it was. If the years could disappear, if everything could be like it was before. . . .

"Yes, we could try again. If you think you can get a holiday, then, fine."

"The fact is," he said with a nervous laugh, "I went to see the doctor about that today."

"About what?"

"Well, I told him how things were—that I feel nervous and upset and that I thought it was the same with you. I didn't say anything about a holiday, of course, but that was when I started thinking about it."

"What did the doctor have to say?"

"Well, he gave me a prescription for some pills."

She looked at him sharply.

"What kind of pills?"

"Tranquillisers of course."

She sat silently for a while.

"What did you intend to use them for?"

"God, what a question," he shouted. "What's the matter with you? Do you think I'd sit here telling you about the pills if I had any ulterior motives? How am I to relax and get my nerves sorted out if you go on like this, these accusations and everlasting suspicions? Are you surprised that I'm nervous, huh? I don't feel well and that's true, but even when I come and confide in you and ask for your help, even when I suggest that we take a holiday and enjoy ourselves, you just sit there all suspicious, with your sinister insinuations. . . ."

"I only asked. God, can't I even ask a question?"

Silence again.

"Well, all right," she said. "I believe you then. You haven't been yourself lately."

He gave her a quick glance and she hastily added:

"I mean, of course, I've noticed that you've been a little run down and irritable. I haven't been feeling too good myself either, you know. Perhaps that's why . . . why I've found it a little difficult to take all that you've done lately. But if you really are ill, then of course. . . ."

"Ill! I'm not ill! I'm overworked and tired and it would all be nothing if only I had a bit of peace and quiet at home and didn't have a wife who keeps on nagging like you do."

"Oh, so I'm to blame for that as well now? That you're so bitter and unkind to me. It's my fault?"

Silence.

"Well, I suppose you're right in a way," she said in a feeble voice. "I suppose it is partly my fault that I'm not as patient as I ought to be. If you want to have a holiday, it's all right by me. It certainly would be nice to go away for a while."

"That's agreed, then," he said and got up from the table. He stood leaning against it, as though something heavy in his legs prevented him from moving.

"I'll ask tomorrow, then," he said.

"Yes, that would be nice."

The question hung in the air.

"If they let you, I can write to Mum and tell her we're going away," she said.

He lifted his weight from the table and left the room.

23

THEY STOOD beside each other in the bedroom looking at his bed.

"Well, this is how I've arranged it. It'll probably be a nice change for you, too, to sleep alone. We might as well sleep like this till we see what happens."

"Yes, of course. Yes." He looked around the room.

"I haven't moved my things out. I suppose I can leave my chest-of-drawers here till we've arranged things a little better. We can always move the bed and the other things out when we know what's going to happen."

"Naturally. I'll help you do it some day."

"Were you thinking of going to bed now?"

He looked at her absent-mindedly.

"Yes, I'm really quite tired. Just thought I'd have a nightcap first. You want one?"

"Is it necessary to drink every night?"

"Of course not. You needn't if you don't want to."

"Perhaps a glass might not be such a bad idea after all," she said softly to him.

"We could always drink to our holiday."

He went downstairs and into the kitchen in front of her. She took the glasses down from the shelf and he fetched a bottle of port.

"I think I'll take one of the pills and see if they're any good," he said.

He took a small medicine bottle out of his pocket and she watched with interest while he opened it and picked out the cotton wool which lay at the top. He tipped two tablets out and put them carefully beside him on the table. Then he took the port and poured them a glass each.

"Cheers."

"Cheers."

They raised their glasses and while she only sipped hers, he emptied his in one go.

"Would you fetch me a glass of water for my pills?"

She opened her mouth but the words didn't get out. 'Why don't you do it yourself? Why should I do it?' she would have said on any other occasion but this. But it would look as though she didn't trust him and the tablets by his side—and she would have to trust him now, if for nothing else but to get some peace and quiet tonight, to avoid having new accusations and more curses flung at her . . . she would trust him. She had to. He might be sincere this time. They were good friends and their nerves were worn. They were both tired but soon they would go away on holiday; it was only natural that a tired husband should ask his wife to fetch him a glass of water, and that she should do it.

She got up slowly, walked up to the cupboard and took out a glass, turned the tap and let the water run for a while before she filled the glass with cold water. She had a sip to see if the water was cold enough, poured a bit out so that the glass wasn't too full, all this deliberately without turning her head.

When she turned around he had placed two tablets on his tongue and the bottle had disappeared into his pocket.

"Here you are."

He drank deeply before he answered.

"Thank you."

24

"Goodnight, then."

"Goodnight."

They were standing on the landing outside their rooms, looking each other in the eye.

"You needn't wake me tomorrow," he said. "Since I'm sleeping alone I might as well keep the alarm clock myself."

"If you like. You can call me later."

As she walked into her room he said:

"By the way, do you know where the key to my room has gone to?"

"No. How should I know? I don't even know if there ever was one. I don't remember ever having locked the door. Why do you ask?"

"Oh, I was just wondering."

"Strange, if you ask me. Why would you want to lock the door?"

"I didn't say I wanted to lock it. I just wondered where the key was. Can't I even ask a simple question?"

"Well, at any rate, I don't know where it is. Sleep well now."

"Sleep well."

She went into her room and turned the light on. There was no shade on the bulb in there and the light fell clear and hard on the rubbish in the room. She sighed and began to undress. There was no key for this

97

room either. But he wouldn't come in. He really had looked tired, and as he'd taken two sleeping tablets no doubt he'd fall asleep quickly.

She felt tired herself, exhausted in a way. She took off her clothes and her body bulged out freely. She stood there and looked sadly at it. Too late. Too late. Or was it? No other man would want her body; it might be tolerable when she wore a girdle and a bra, but as she stood there alone looking at it she knew that it was too late—too late for most things. Oh, if it were only true that they were going on holiday, that everything would be all right again. It wouldn't be much, no, she wouldn't gain much, but at least it would be better than going on the way it had been, for God knows how long....

A tiny flame flickered through her, a tiny desire to go into his room and cuddle up in his bed. But what if he didn't want her?—then everything would start all over again, and even worse. It felt quite good now, as though there was a little hope. She would have liked to lie close to him now; normally it was all right as long as she turned her face away from him; for if she smelt his breath nothing would work, that sour stale smell, often with a sting of alcohol mixed in it ... she had sometimes lain beside him, her eyes closed, and had managed to forget about the smell, managed to pretend that it wasn't him.

That it was a young man, a handsome man with a strong, lithe body, not too much fat anywhere; narrow hips and strong arms, a man with dark, wavy hair and clear blue eyes and a body that was strong, firm, clean, with hard muscles which tore in to her, worked on her and made themselves felt all over her body ... quite the opposite from what she was used to. Didn't they say that young men were often attracted to older women? Only she never met anyone, had no contact with anyone. But to a young man she would be something, would be able to give something . . . her hands followed the contours of her body, lifted and pressed the floppy skin. If she could lie there beside him with her eyes closed pretending he was someone else. So tired. So tired. It was as though she wasn't really herself, couldn't keep her thoughts clear. Was it only the port . . . ?

The medicine bottle he had put into his pocket! The sediment on the bottom of her glass! He had asked her for a glass of water and she had given it him, had turned her face away to show that she trusted him, that she would give him another chance to prove that he was honest. She had believed him and he had laid a trap for her! How many? How strong? How soon?

25

HE TURNED heavily in bed and tried to force himself to
sleep. Oh, damn this! Damn! He had just taken two
tablets, had even demonstratively showed her that he
had taken two tablets, and yet—were they only sleeping
pills that bloody doctor had given him? He didn't
know how long he had been lying like this but it felt
like ages and sleep hadn't come. He ought to be able
to sleep. He had nothing to be afraid of tonight. He
had lulled the old woman into believing she was safe,
she wouldn't do anything to him now; he had shown
her that his intentions were sincere and that he meant
well. He'd been sitting there by the table with the bottle
in his hand, had even asked her to fetch him some water
to give himself a chance to fiddle with her glass—yet
he had taken the two tablets himself as she must have
seen before he had stuffed the bottle into his pocket
again.

She should feel ashamed of herself when thinking
about it—mean and suspicious as she had been as
usual, even threatening him with her old Mum, claim-
ing that she was afraid of him, that he was trying to
do away with her! No, he'd show her now. He'd show
her that it had all been in her sick imagination only
and then she would feel ashamed, weak as she was. It
was a wonder she hadn't come sneaking into his room
and cuddled up to him like she normally did when he

was the least bit friendly towards her. Just for that it was worth shouting at the old hag and especially in the evenings; he couldn't bear having her hands caressing him and feeling how she pressed and pushed her floppy body against his. Well, she probably wouldn't do it tonight since it would spoil her little game with the bed.

He laughed loudly to himself. There she was lying in the lumber-room, on the floor, surrounded by old sweaty socks she had been too lazy to wash and darn; it served her right! Let her lie in the filth. At least he had made her think differently, and think honestly. She ought to be tame by now. She had probably imagined that he'd try to put some pills into her glass—how baffled she'd get when she realised that he hadn't. Bloody frightened she'd be at first, and then she'd see later that she'd been outwitted again. How ashamed she'd be. He was convinced she'd write to the old woman first thing tomorrow and take it all back, explain she'd made a mistake, she had such a kind, good husband really. Better than she deserved, the old witch.

Perhaps he'd been a bit too rash about that telegram. He wasn't sure; it had seemed like a good idea at the time. Put a bit of fright into the old bag. Not let her feel too confident while she was fiddling with her poisons, make her think that others kept watch on her. Make her a little more careful about what she gave him to eat. It would look bad if something really did happen to him and someone else had sent the telegram. She would never, ever, be quite sure.

But now he felt he had the situation under control. The wife was docile now and lay there feeling conscience-stricken because she'd thought badly about him. That would keep her from being too tricky for a while. Especially that one about a holiday! She'd been suspicious in the beginning, oh, yes. She hadn't believed him, had thought it was only talk, that he just wanted to soften her up before he aimed his final blow. But she hadn't thought as far ahead as he, that was her big mistake—she was unable to grasp the situation as a whole. He could safely make plans now, be nice and kind to her, pretend that he was sorry about their little misunderstandings.

Perhaps he might even succeed in wheedling out of her the letter he'd written. It was too bad that he'd agreed to writing that. He'd just been thinking that he'd get her letter. Well, he'd simply keep working on her for another couple of days and then it would be as easy as anything to make her give it to him. He could claim that he'd lost the one she gave him, or thrown it away at work. It was only a joke after all, he'd never intended to keep it—surely she hadn't thought that he'd go around keeping something like that? Best if she gave him back his; after all, sweetie, we'll be going on holiday shortly and we'll have such a nice time. They might as well go on holiday, and then when they came home he'd be able to do whatever he wanted, she would trust him fully. Then would be the time for the tablets to come out again to fulfil their little mission. Right now, he'd rest sweetly with his own clean little conscience, rest—sleep.

26

SHE MUST not sleep. That was the most important thing. *She must not sleep.* If only she knew how many he'd given her. Well, there couldn't have been room for too many in that small port glass and he couldn't have had time to put in very many and stir them too. She could hardly die from a few sleeping tablets. But perhaps he'd wanted to give her just enough to make her sleep heavily so that he could come later on and finish off the job in some other way. She had first thought of taking something to make her vomit, mustard in hot water was supposed to be good, or just two fingers in the throat. But it might have been too late already by then. And he might hear her and come and prevent her.

She didn't know if he was asleep or whether he'd been up himself vomiting, he could have done it without her hearing, unsuspicious as she was, she wouldn't have noticed if he had already got up and been sick in the toilet. She couldn't remember whether he had or not. Perhaps he was lying awake just waiting for her to fall asleep and then later on he'd sneak in and . . . but it wouldn't be as easy as that, oh no, little man, I've got you where I want you. So he thought he could get round her, did he? Sitting there with all his false talk about a holiday, and me thinking he was going on about it just so that I wouldn't ask Mum to stay. Oh no! His plans are bigger, but this time he has outwitted himself; I'm not trapped so easily.

She couldn't just sit here all night fighting sleep. God knows how many he'd given her, maybe four or five tablets at least—there was enough room for them in the glass. She'd have to do something so she didn't fall asleep, she couldn't rely on her willpower alone. Black coffee would help, that was certain. She would have to sneak down into the kitchen and put the coffee on and then just drink gallons of it. She would also have a cigarette. She couldn't sit in here smoking, the smell would still be hanging about tomorrow morning even if she aired the room and it would look strange. But it would be all right in the kitchen where he usually smoked. Hadn't he been sitting there puffing away all night?

She would first smoke four or five and mess up the ashtray—or rather the saucer, that was more like him—and then later she'd start work. He wouldn't even have time to wake and find out what had happened to him. And especially since he had those sleeping tablets inside him, him who never used to take any medicine. It would of course be better if she could sit in his bedroom smoking but she didn't dare do that. He might wake up and then she'd be stuck without any means of escape—'I wanted so much to sit here and look at you my dear, be near you and yet not disturb you, and then I had a few cigarettes just to keep me awake'—no, that sounded too silly, he'd never fall for that one. She'd have to go and smoke in the kitchen, although it was only the next best solution. But it'd be all right. The plan was foolproof, if only he was asleep first.

She tiptoed across the floor to the door and listened.

Not a sound. She stepped soundlessly on to the landing, and walked up to his door, putting her ear to it. She heard some noises from inside, heard him turning over; he muttered something and snored loudly, but he often did that in his sleep, he was probably falling into a deep sleep now.

Or was he wide awake and making those noises just to hoodwink her? No, he couldn't know she was standing there. He must think that she was fast asleep after all that lot he had poured into her. No doubt he intended to sleep off the effect of the pills before he went into her room do what he had in mind. He had the alarm clock after all, he had made sure of that; yet another cunning trick that he had wrapped up in the disguise of friendliness and thoughtfulness. Oh, as she was standing there she felt a wild urge to go in and put her hands round his neck and twist it—yes, just twist it, no silly nonsense about pressing it—but to take a good hold of his head and simply turn it till his tongue and eyes hung out of his head. To go in and twist . . . to sit down on him, sit on him till he choked, oh, what a heavenly feeling; press all life out of him—after all he'd done to her, press the evil and cunning out of his body . . . but it was only thoughts. Only wishful thinking and self-indulgence. It would happen much more easily than that, much more precisely, much more safely, much less dangerously for her.

27

OH, GOD, her head. How many tablets had he slipped into her glass? It couldn't have been so very many. After all she hadn't noticed a different taste when she drank the port, the glass was so small, there couldn't have been room for much in it, and she hadn't seen any . . . the sediment at the bottom! She had thought it was the port, but of course it had been the tablets! Still it couldn't have been more than a couple, no more than he'd thought sufficient to send her to sleep, a deep sleep so that he'd have the time he needed. He thought she was asleep now, probably he was now lying there waiting for her or was just about to get up himself.

He'd go into her room and look for her and—God! if he found the bed empty and started hunting for her! He'd be furious, insane that he hadn't succeeded; he'd look for her, find her in the kitchen, start hitting her and swearing . . . realise that she'd found out about his plan. He'd ask why she was sitting there smoking and not lying in bed; she would of course play the innocent, but what could she say? Agree with him, not let him know, hide her thoughts from him, 'oh dear, my head felt so heavy, what if I've eaten something bad or the port was too strong for me, I really don't feel well, had a cup of coffee and a cigarette to clear my head. . . .'

Two cigarettes were alight. It was the cigarettes that had made her so dizzy, too. She didn't know how to smoke really. She had never smoked before except for once when she was a young girl and had wanted to try it, but the taste had been foul and her Dad had found out and said that it was terrible to see young girls smoking, that it was dangerous for the body and that one might stop growing; she had never smoked again. She wouldn't have done it even if her father hadn't said anything for the taste had been so disgusting and she had got a headache from it. It was the same now. She heaved the smoke in slowly between her lips and let it out immediately. He always inhaled; she had tried that too for she wasn't certain if the cigarette end would reveal whether she had done so or not, and it would be a bit of a blow if they examined the stubs afterwards and found that the person who'd smoked them hadn't inhaled. But there didn't seem to be any difference and she wouldn't have been able to do it anyway—it felt as though her heart was going to stop, as though her blood was congealing in the veins; she could see dark spots before her tear-filled eyes.

She had had to curl up to suppress her need to cough. She couldn't even bear to think about how people could smoke, how he could smoke and think that it was nice. He probably did it only to annoy her for he knew how much she detested the smell of cigarettes. Pleasant-smelling cigars he wouldn't touch, of course. Nor a pipe. And one could get cancer from smoking the stuff, too. She had told him that but he had laughed at her and thought she was stupid. Well, maybe it wasn't too late for him to fall ill yet. Or rather it wouldn't have been too late, if he had been a little nicer to her and if he hadn't tried to do what he did the other night. He could have had many years left to fall ill and die. But he had made his own choice. It was all his fault that she was sitting here smoking, feeling utterly sick in her desperate, helpless attempt to save her life. . . . Three cigarettes. Small, small puffs then letting the smoke out quickly again.

Three cigarette ends in the saucer would be enough surely? After all, he never used to lie in bed smoking. Would it look suspicious? She ought to have taken the alarm clock while she was at it. She'd have to take it as soon as she got upstairs again. First get the alarm clock and turn it off and then sneak back in again and do what she had to do. If only she could be certain that he was fast asleep, so that he didn't suddenly wake up because of the smoke and put out the fire and realise what had happened. Then she'd be in it up to her neck, absolutely, and not just on the brink like she had been until now. If that happened she might as well take her own life at once, for he'd call the police.

She ought to try and get hold of his sleeping tablets as well so that she could take them in case he woke up. That should prevent him from having her put away. How he'd laugh if that happened, really enjoy himself. . . . But he must be asleep. He had taken two sleeping tablets, taken them deliberately. She had seen it herself, in that respect there had been no hanky-panky. Oh, if only she had the tablets. Then she might even be able to slip a few tablets into his mouth while he was asleep, and still have enough left to make it safe for her just in case . . . but she didn't dare. It was too bold. They could get stuck in his throat and he'd start coughing while she was doing it. Useless.

She puffed on the fourth cigarette and got up,

trembling. She wanted to relax, wanted so much to unwind. All that she'd been thinking, all that she'd been sitting there planning had, after all, been only dreams— it had been like something she had read, really nothing at all to do with her. Careless smoker suffocated in bed— wife in despair: 'I ought to have woken up, I ought to have looked after him better, I told him time and time again but he wouldn't listen!' She saw it as in a film. No, no, she had never really seriously thought of doing it. She would pour water on the burning cigarette ends and throw them in the dustbin and then go to sleep again. She was so tired, so tired.

She felt that she must sleep, and it wasn't only because of the sleeping tablets she felt like that, no, it was something inside her that was so tired that it couldn't stay awake, she just couldn't keep her eyes open. To go to sleep and then wake and be young and happy again as she had been, be with a nice man, wake up to a new world, a new future. It wasn't too late yet.

She'd go up and wake him, talk to him and . . . no, it was no good. She couldn't, didn't dare, she couldn't trust him any longer. He'd only agree with her in everything she said; 'Now old girl, what kind of nightmares have you been having, you go to sleep again, don't forget I have to get up in the morning, don't sit here nattering all night for God's sake', and he would pat her or hit her depending on which feeling was strongest in him and she'd never get to know what he really thought, what he really felt deep inside. No, she'd have to act now, quickly, while she still had the opportunity. Otherwise she'd be greeted by his sour looks in the morning and wonder how, when, where? . . . Not have anywhere to go, no money, be alone with him. She'd have to do it, quickly, quickly before she began thinking too much about it again and before she got frightened and scared, quickly while she still had the power and the courage, before he woke up, quickly before she started to cry.

She didn't dare. She couldn't do it. If only she could sit here, like him the night before, sleeping with her arms on the table; but he might come down tomorrow morning and find her. . . . The bottle with paint-thinner in the cupboard. . . . What if he knew it was there, remembered it. . . . It couldn't go on like this. Not like this for ever. She'd have to do something. It wasn't her fault. Hadn't she always tried, done her best to be a good wife, subordinated herself to his needs, let him decide, put up with him and tried to be what he wanted, but how long, God, how long can a woman go on. . . . ? A woman needs encouragement, needs love to be able to go on! But his everlasting quarrelling, his fits of rage, his lack of affection and kindness . . . it wasn't her fault.

She couldn't help it, she had just been a young girl and not known how difficult it would be, she wasn't to know then that she had married the wrong man. She had sacrificed so much for his sake, and now it was too late to change it. Now she was stuck with him, too old, too tired, too worn out to break loose and try again. Here she was all alone in the kitchen in the middle of the night, not even daring to go up to bed because he was lying up there waiting for her, wanting to kill her. This was how things were. It wasn't she who wanted it, it was self-defence, it was he who had forced her to it, she had to think about herself sometimes, and not just about him all the time, some time she'd have to put herself before everything else!

With trembling hands she picked up the saucer with the four smouldering stubs, and with the fifth cigarette in her mouth, she walked upstairs.

28

He woke up in a blanket of smoke. Fog, mist, smoke that rose out of nothing and swirled in over him from above, as though there was a hole in the roof and heavy mists came billowing in from a stormy sky out there, or as though they were spat out of every corner, made of nothing but old dust and cobwebs rolled forward, big and grey and ensnaring, huge cobwebs followed by a lazy heat and a heavy closeness, deeper.... He woke, but not properly. The cobweb and the dust was in his head and his body, made his lungs tired, prevented his eyes from opening. Something from above forced itself into him and yet at the same time it seemed to come from below, it pressed on him from both sides and left him no room to stretch, to breathe, to open his eyes and see the light. Dark it was, dark, grey and black in changing nuances, he couldn't discern it properly, yet he knew that it was on him, surrounding him, it was on its way down under the blanket, about to enfold his body like a grey wrapping, and at the same time it moved in the air, its grey and burning belly turned up, exposing to his sight underneath something that looked like a sharp fin, like a shark's, narrow and sharp....

But it was soft, soft just the same, the animal in his room. It whirled about silently, it was toothless and smelt so strange, it must be dead. A dead whale maybe, that turned about in the air like it would have done in water, just as though the air had been water, resistant, tenacious and billowy. The whale was rotting in the still water, and then it had begun to sink, to disintegrate. Despite its vast bulk it was soft as a cloud, but heavy, choking. . . .

If only he could wake up. If only he could open his eyes and see what it was, this huge, silent, grey animal, but it was as though this animal, the smell, the heat, the smoke, the cloud—the rotting flesh—was forcing its way into his eyes, making him close them tighter, making him slide further down under the covers, deeper, as far down as he could, where he couldn't be reached, where the animal couldn't touch him. He knew he was in his own bed; he ought to be safe. Nothing could happen to him here. Not in his own bed. He had had some peculiar thoughts, a fear had come over him when he had looked into his wife's eyes or read over her shoulder, an exciting feeling of danger and at the same time of life, adventure; something was happening at last, something was touching his strings.

But not in this way, not sneaking into his own bed; he was safe here after all, he remembered his thoughts from before he fell asleep and they told him that he was safe. They had calmed him down and said time, time is yours, relax, sleep, you're in your own bed, the future and freedom are in your hands but you must keep it up . . . but when had he thought that? Was it very long ago? Had the time already come, stayed and watched him sleep, and then gone again leaving him alone? Had he let time slip like grains of sand between his fingers while he was asleep, while this monster, this eyeless animal, this huge dead thing had sneaked over him to strangle him? He didn't know, time didn't exist, only the room was left and in it this something that engulfed him.

Then he saw it before him, his wife's face. It smiled towards him, smiled in a way it hadn't done for a long time. He saw the smile whirling around and changing, huge shiny eyeteeth were protruding, it changed into a grimace, but came back again submissive and mild like before. He stretched out his arm to feel her, her smile had made him remember times that had been, how she had looked then. Perhaps time hadn't stopped or gone by but had instead gone back, taken him back to a time long ago when it still hadn't been too late . . . when a body had lain next to him in bed, young and warm and firm, with no flabby white flesh, firm and lithe, something to hold, something to bite, a firm body. Now, he needed it now, if only he could keep it tight . . . through the mists that surrounded him he felt something grow between his legs to become big and stiff, he felt the warmth spread through his body even up into his face: he was full of expectation, he had been given another chance and it still wasn't too late. He could do it! He wanted to! He'd show her, yes, he would, he'd make her feel that he was still a man! His hand was moving, searching between the sheets towards the other side of the bed; his body followed, it turned on its side, half raised to the right height to take hold of her and disappear into her. . . .

It was empty. Empty. Empty. He tore his eyes open and felt the muscle spasms. And despite the stinging pain and the tears in his eyes, tears of deceit, pain and bad temper, he could see that her bed was empty. And the cloud was smoke, the animal, the dead whale was also smoke and grey shadows. It came from him—the smoke. From his own bed it rose towards the ceiling and turned halfway up, pressing against the walls. . . .

He was up with one leap.

29

Now, now he had her. Now he knew. He knew. He laughed loudly as he stood by the bed, piling on more and more blankets to stop the fire. A feeling that resembled triumph, happiness overwhelmed him—he wanted to laugh and scream. It was like stepping into the sunlight after being in a long tunnel with dust and filth in his hair. He had her now. It hadn't yet started burning properly but his mattress was smouldering; the cigarette stubs she had put there had burnt a hole right through the sheet and partly through the mattress where it would have started to flare up soon—if he hadn't woken up in time, if he hadn't seen her face.

He did not know whether he really had seen her face, grinning towards him; he had thought it was a dream or some kind of fantasy but it could have been her, the real living her who had stood by his bed smiling gently for fear of waking him so that she'd be forced to explain why she was standing there. Only she hadn't managed to conceal her real self and her scornful smile had prevailed. There had been a face only, no body . . . no, it couldn't have been her but her evil spirit which had been there to watch him die, so that it could fly through the air with a witch's shriek to report to her afterwards. Now he was awake. She was gone.

There wasn't as much smoke in the room as he had felt when he had been half asleep; what he had seen must have been a warning from within himself. But it was smoke he had seen on the ceiling, grey and dirty, the whole room had been filled with it and he couldn't stop the cough that kept rising in his throat, too srong to be kept back by willpower; it would have made him explode. He must be poisoned. One didn't burn to death but was poisoned by the smoke. He could have lain there dying slowly, have crept deeper and deeper down under the blankets until the monster had sat on him with its fat arse and squashed the life out of him. On his bedside table was the saucer with four cigarette stubs in it. She was cunning, the bitch! What a devil. She had even thought about leaving evidence of him having smoked in bed!

This deceit of hers was the lowest, the filthiest, the most base so far. She had been lying awake in her bed, knowing that he didn't want to do her any harm, knowing that he had taken the tablets and would sleep soundly, realising that she could now feel safe in her home with him, that all her suspicions had been evil fantasies, fostered in her sick, confused brain. And then she had got up and. . . . Her evil was greater than he had ever thought possible. How was it possible to defend oneself against such wickedness? What could one do other than hit out blindly in an attempt to save one's own life? As he stood there putting out the fire he was overcome by a feeling of satisfaction, a deep feeling of contentment. It was as though *he* was killing *her*; his satisfaction was greater than it would have been had she really been in the bed with him and he had taken her.

He could let it burn. Yes, he might as well let it burn, feed the fire to make it flare up, open the window before

117

it died completely. He could go into her room and hit her hard with something that wouldn't leave a mark, his bare hands for example, and carry her into the bedroom afterwards and put her on the bed—how clever! How clever of her to move out of the room tonight. He could set fire to the bed again, let the smoke flare up like it had done before, and rush out on to the landing himself, horrified and out of his wits while she lay there suffocating in her own evil.

He couldn't rouse her, had thought she was already dead. He had shaken her and tried to wake her but she hadn't moved. Or he had thought that she had woken before him and was on her way out of the house, not seen that she was still in the bed. He had been panic-stricken, and was horrified now that he realised what had happened. If he had only thought of carrying her out of the room and not just tried to rouse her, but he was half-unconscious himself, hadn't known what he was doing. Yes, it was true, he had been smoking in bed. If only he hadn't. And she had warned him so often that this might happen one day. As though he hadn't been warned. But one always thinks that kind of thing never happens to oneself. . . . He'd never smoke again, never.

Or, no—it was better if she had been smoking, it would have to have been her if he was to go free. It was she who had been smoking in bed and fallen asleep with a burning cigarette in her hand. No, that was no good after all, she never smoked. They'd find that out easily, and what would they say then? But what if she'd done it just this once? How was he to know, he was asleep after all? Damn it, it was her who had smoked, that was the worst part of it, it wasn't him, yet everybody would think it was. She really had thought that one out, the bitch. There was no way of getting out of it for him. They would come and ask: Who's been smoking in bed? Well, it wasn't him. So, it was her?

No, she loathed the smell of cigarettes, that was well known. *'Pardon me, madam, did madam smoke in bed last night, madam who usually doesn't smoke? Should we believe what your spouse says or should we believe what sounds more plausible, namely that he had lied about the fire as well as about saving you later; perhaps we'd better have a closer look at this case....'* 'Yes, constable, it was my husband and him alone, if the constable only knew how many times I've told him that ...'* there was no way out. Even after her death her voice would rise from the shadows and talk and have him condemned. Was she awake now, waiting outside the door? Was she wondering if he were dead yet, did she maybe think that the noise she heard was his death rattle? The devil take you, you bitch, if you're sitting there you'll have the surprise of your lifetime, your last surprise for that matter! Or was she asleep in her bed, slumbering sweetly after a good day's work? Was she dreaming of the money he had in the bank?

He made sure that the fire was extinguished, that not one single spark was alive. Then he went to open the window and stood there leaning with both hands against the window sill, looking out on to the dark garden.

30

SHE HAD gone back to bed as soon as it was done, had pulled the sheets over her head and crept down in the bed. Stiff as a board she lay there, wide awake, waiting. She held a conversation with herself, but silently, inside her head. No! I haven't done anything! I'm only thinking that I did it! I was sitting in the kitchen smoking and planning but I never did it. I'm not that kind of a person. It was only silly thoughts, fantasies. I never really contemplated doing it. I only thought about it to amuse myself, just a diversion; it wasn't serious. She hadn't done it. She was sure she hadn't done it. She hadn't tiptoed into his room, holding her breath, crept step by step on silent feet till she'd reached his bed and stood looking at him; seen him lying there, sweaty, his hair untidy, snoring, open-mouthed, his sheets already curled up and messy around him, a hairy leg sticking out by the foot end.

No, she had just stood there looking at him, taken a few more steps towards the bed, picked up the alarm quietly, turned it off. She had only gone in there to get the alarm clock and put it in her own room, so that she could make sure she got up before him, so that she could have the coffee going while he got dressed, so that he wouldn't have to get up on his own, to do him a favour. She hadn't had a saucer in her hand, no burning cigarette in her mouth. Or had she? No. And even if she had, she wasn't sure any more, but had a faint recollection of cigarettes playing a role somewhere. She was sure she had gone back into the kitchen and emptied the saucer, washed it and put the cigarettes back on the shelf where he used to keep his—or had *she?*

Where had she put the packet of cigarettes? Cold sweat appeared on her body, dampening her night-dress, and also her armpits. Where had she put it? Should she go down and have a look? Was it still on the kitchen table? Well, even if there was a packet of cigarettes on the kitchen table that really wasn't any reason to get up. He'd just forgotten to put them away. Fingerprints! Her fingerprints! She must get rid of them—No, no, there must be some left, his fingerprints ought to be on it as well. She'd have to throw the packet away. In fact, she ought to be in the kitchen now, fetching the cigarettes and then flushing them away in the toilet, burn the packet itself—but she didn't dare, her body was absolutely paralysed, she couldn't move. She must get up and go to the kitchen but she couldn't leave the bed. It was like a cocoon, she lay rolled in the sheets like a chrysalis, she had no wings yet, couldn't fly....

No! She hadn't done it! She had just been watching him and then gone out again. She had never put the saucer on his bedside table and put the burning cigarette in his bed, under the top sheet quite near his hand so that it really would look as though it had fallen out of his hand; that had been the worst part! She would much rather have put it by his feet, just have let it fall and then fled. It hadn't really been dangerous, just a joke, to frighten him a little—or had she actually put it in his bed, near his hand, near his face? Had she? Had she?

I must go and have a look. God, what am I thinking about? I must be mad. I couldn't have done such a thing. I'm just imagining it. Like when one goes out and suddenly gets the notion that one has forgotten to turn the iron or the cooker off, and makes a complete fool of oneself, rushing back to check, everybody laughs; it's an obsession. You get home and find that both the iron and the cooker are turned off. You go through a thousand rituals to make absolutely sure that it really is so—say loudly to yourself that now you've turned off the cooker, and press the plug for the iron hard against your hand so that it leaves a mark as proof long after, but as soon as you are out in the street again the thought returns: Did I really? Didn't I when checking turn the switch on again? And it goes on and on, like that. She could go back to his room again, just sneak across the landing and open the door slightly to make sure that he was lying there as usual, talking and snoring in his sleep, turning so that the sheets got tangled round him more and more. He would lie there like a big pig, just as he always did. And she'd go back into her own room and laugh at herself.

She hadn't taken his tablets. There. Hadn't she thought of taking his tablets, yet hadn't done it? So, she couldn't have done the other things either. Oh, if only she had the tablets now! Just one pill so that she could get some sleep, to put an end to these idiotic thoughts. She had only gone there to get the alarm clock to help him get up in the morning—that was all! She stretched out on her bed; after having lain curled up for a while her legs had got cramp, they felt absolutely paralysed, hard and numb. She'd have to get up and move about. Just open the window and breathe some fresh air.

There was a strange smell from somewhere, but that might be her imagination too. It couldn't be true since nothing was burning in the house, she had finished all the cigarettes she had smoked, not left any. . . . Or had she forgotten to pour water on them? Fires could happen if one did that, she had often read about burning cigarettes in wastepaper baskets—didn't she have a note about it in her book? The book, so long ago— she'd have to go down to the kitchen to see if everything was all right. She wasn't sure if she'd turned the light off either; perhaps it was burning down there, and she didn't know if she had closed the cellar door properly. She'd have to go down and have a look. I can sleep afterwards. I can go to his room afterwards and take a tablet out of the bottle and then sleep all night. I must be going mad the way I'm lying here imagining things and day-dreaming.

She got out of bed and was forced to lean against the wall in order not to fall. She felt a lump in her throat that prevented her from swallowing. It was exhaustion that overwhelmed her now and made her dizzy, but she'd have to go down and check. . . . Up to the door, leaning against the wall. Open the door. Oh! That smell, something was smelling—it wasn't the dustbin down there, nor the dirty socks in the lumber-room either. . . . Oh God, what had she done? . . . No, no, no, not her, someone else had done it! Perhaps he'd taken the packet of cigarettes up with him and had lain in bed smoking after she had been in his room. . . .

She stood on the landing, her head leaning against

the wall, but couldn't take one more step, felt that she had to sit down if she wasn't going to fall. Then she heard that he was awake, that he was coughing, that he suddenly began to laugh. And as though someone had put ice on her head the pain of realisation now went through her whole body: It is true! It has happened! I'm alone! I have done it and he knows. And he's alive!

31

SHE STOOD there unable to move, but felt how tears came to her eyes. It was as though she was standing beside the crying woman who leaned helplessly against the wall, observing her. Her whole body was trembling, her tears ran wild and uncontrolled down her face without her even raising her hands to wipe them away, and just the same this woman was unable to move an inch. Come, she wanted to say. Come and kill me, I'm waiting. I'm only a few yards away and I can't manage to walk one more step. Kill me, I haven't got the energy to wait. Put an end to it. Don't laugh. Don't wait any longer. Come and kill me so that I won't have to play this game any more. I can't manage it. I'm not strong enough.

His feet were moving on the floor in there; it was as though she heard everything through a loudspeaker, the sound was amplified—it was as though a herd of huge elephants came slowly trampling through a desert, a long row, every one with the trunk wound round the tail of the one in front. . . . And she stood there pressed against the wall and couldn't move while the elephants came closer and closer, they just marched forward, heading straight for her, tumbled right over. . . . His steps were not directed towards the door; he wouldn't come and get her, not yet; she was still meant to stand here trembling with the tears falling in a meaningless stream down her face. He had walked up to the window now and opened it. The fire must have been put out.

Yet again the ice went through her like a sword: Am I going mad? Am I dreaming, can this be true? Am I standing on the landing in just a nightdress waiting for my husband to come and kill me, because he's realised that I've tried to kill him? No, no, not yet! It wasn't meant seriously; she hadn't succeeded, he wasn't dead after all. I haven't really done anything, I was only playing a joke on him, of course I'm fond of him. But I know what he'll think, he can never see anything except from his own point of view, it'll be no use trying to reason with him, not this time. . . . Oh, I dare not see him, he's in there now, absolutely quiet, laughing and chuckling to himself, it must mean that he's thought of something, he's thought up some way of revenging himself. Am I sane, just standing here waiting for him? How long have I been standing here? Five minutes? Ten? Giving him time. Any minute now he might come storming out, see me standing here and just reach out a hand and . . . no! Help! He mustn't kill me, it can't be true, it can't be!

She saw beside her the other woman, a middle-aged, slightly comical woman in a long thin nightdress; saw her stumbling towards the stairs to hurry down them. The woman bent forward to get a hold of the banisters, both her hands clasped it, and as she did so, she stumbled forward and caught her foot in a bit of her nightdress and it looked as though she was falling. . . .

Now she was crying, without worrying about it being heard. It's the stairs. He's done something to them. When could he have done it? He is everywhere, sees everything, I'm alone. I must get out of here. He must have put something on the stairs or put a string across them. She had fallen to her knees on one of the first steps and her foot had been caught in something, he must have heard it, she was crying all the time now, heard her own heaving and sobbing, could hardly see anything because of the tears that filled her eyes. Up again; she lifted the nightdress above her knees with one hand, then stormed down the rest of the stairs; the foot she had hurt gave way under her and a sharp pain ran through her whole leg, but she stumbled on, jumped while she fell, only the banisters held her up, her feet got tangled in each other like threads of cotton.

She heard a sound behind her and looked up; saw the beam of light from his door growing. He was coming after her. She stumbled forward through the dark hall, she must get down there, out in the street, and jump and scream and cry, she'd have to scream if she wasn't to be choked. She heard this woman mutter some prayers to God and to her mother, while she fought forward in the blinding darkness. In her frenzy she felt drips between her legs. The garage. If only I stand still so that he can't hear me. If only I can make him go past me without seeing me down here. I must get into the garage. He knows I can't drive so he won't think that I've tried to hide in there. He'll think I've tried to hide down here, or rush out into the street. I must get down into the basement and into the garage while he's looking for me here. He'll go into the street and have a look, but while he's outside I can get back and get my coat and bag and a pair of shoes, and then back to the garage and later I'll sneak out and go and see Mum; he'll never dare report me to the police, he'll know that everyone will laugh at him because he's so stupid and ridiculous, and he knows that I can tell a few things too. . . .

Quickly and silently she had turned the corner by the basement door. Now he was already in the hall and turned on the light. The light! He'd turn on all the lights and look for her! Or perhaps not; she had a feeling that he wouldn't dare look for her in full light; he'd sooner get hold of her in the dark, and hit her and kick her and tear her, yes, she knew, she hoped it would be like that. . . . He was in the kitchen now, he turned the light on and then off again, but meanwhile she had hidden behind the basement door and was now on her way down the stairs, fighting her way to the garage door through the rubbish. Get in there . . . under the car . . on the back seat, in the luggage compartment, just in case he decided to come and have a look there. Not that he ever would, he'd just look from the door, then go. She must make herself invisible. The garage, the car, the back seat, down on the floor. Safe.

32

He almost had to laugh out loud. He could hear the laughter deep inside him, he was so full of it that it wanted to come out through his ears. Oh, he had her now; this was really nice. Scared out of her wits she was now, running through the rooms down there, he heard her sobbing which sounded like an idiot's, heard her stumbling and falling and tripping in her long, ridiculous nightdress he'd always had such a bloody time try to get it off and sorted out. He had almost giggled himself to death when she had stumbled on the stairs and nearly fallen flat on her face—that would have been a beautiful sight, her lying there flat out on the floor with her bare arse in just the right position to be kicked—what a sight!

He had deliberately stopped up there by the stairs to give her a little leeway, it would be so much nicer that way, chasing her from room to room, guided only by a sniff or a squeak that escaped her throat although he knew that she'd be swallowing time and time again to suppress it. She'd hit against the furniture, knock her toes against something and then give a little squeak that she would think he hadn't heard—all the time he'd let her have a little leeway to make her think she was safe, he'd do it all night. Oh, what fun! He'd give her back what she deserved. He might even manage to scare the life out of her; that was one of the things she had noted down in her little book, one could just say 'boo' to old heart-troubled bitches and they'd fall dead on the spot, no proof, all quiet. Well, she always had had a weak heart!

Chase her, he'd chase her. Let her suffer for all those years, for all that chat, quarrelling, for all her cunning and evil, round and round the house he'd drive her till she no longer knew where he was, where she herself was, till she no longer knew from what side to expect him, he'd rush past her quite near, perhaps let his hand touch her, yet not catch hold of her. He'd hardly been able to suppress a laugh when he heard her sobbing and knew that she stood pressed against the wall, her nightdress in her hand—like one holds an evening dress. Her bony white legs with the bad veins shining in the light from a street lamp by the window, see the whites in her eyes moving in the dark, but he wouldn't grab her, not yet, not until she asked him to. Not till she was lying on her knees in sweat and tears and begging him to stop chasing her. . . . What would he do then?

He didn't want that moment to come, wanted the chase to last a long, long time. First the chase. First sneak after her, laughing scornfully in the dark, place himself between her and the front door so that she couldn't get out of the house. No, she was stuck here, she knew that he'd realised who and what she was, her cheap little cowardice and deceit which she'd thought would succeed. Perhaps she had thought that he would have lain in his bed dying slowly from the poisonous fumes and burning in the flames and that she would wake up the next day, a widow—if the whole house had not burnt down, with her and everything; that would have been an unexpected end to the case, the bitch burnt to death herself in the lumber-room, with all the other muck, a punishment, a wonderful punishment for her. . . . But this was better. This would last longer. This was much more fun for him. (Oh, how triumphant he felt.)

His heart rejoiced; he was young again, a strong, invincible Tarzan chasing a wounded wild boar, a stupid noisy boar that trampled along, getting itself more and more entangled in the undergrowth and branches while the young Tarzan moved quickly and silently in the shadows, the spear in his raised hand, his lips slightly apart and his thoughts on the warm meat. . . .

He knew exactly where she was all the time. She thought she was sneaking around silently, thought he had lost track of her, perhaps she even thought she'd make it, get away and hide herself before he threw the spear. Let her! Let her run a little longer! He could hear her moving in the darkness behind him while he himself went into the kitchen and turned on the light, making a big fuss of pretending to look for her. Ha! Ha! She was standing out there in the corridor. Through the noise in the kitchen, the opening and closing of the cupboard doors, he heard her exhausted breathing outside somewhere behind him. This was a wonderful night, pure pleasure! To raise his voice and call out for her, to turn on the light in the hall and see her, would be to spoil everything; it would mean having her around, being forced to act and speak, to ask for explanations, quarrel with her. He wanted no words, just this splendid silence, silence broken only by a few gasps and heavings behind him. This was wonderful, manhood rushed in the boiling blood through his veins, coloured his face and filled his mouth with a strong irresistible taste of blood.

33

HER HEART beat less rapidly after she had been lying for a while on the floor in the back of the car; her body was drying and began to feel cold. She breathed more regularly, her sobbing was less convulsive. He wouldn't come. He would never find her here. He would never guess that she had hidden here. He was too stupid. He couldn't think further than he could see. She really had fooled him. He'd gone right into the kitchen, like the simple-minded monkey he was. As though she would have hidden there! Hadn't he even opened the door of the broom-cupboard. As though he thought she could have been hiding between the brooms and mops—that would have been a sight, she could have hit him on the head with a brush! She licked up the snot that had run from her nose and giggled hoarsely to herself. He'd never look here.

But she couldn't stay here all night. He'd come in the morning and start the car and go to work. How could she have been so stupid as to even think about hiding in the car? In the car! It had seemed the right thing to do, the only place she could think of, a private place where nobody could see her; it was safer than standing in a dark corner somewhere in the house, hearing him coming nearer and nearer and not being able to stop sobbing, waiting for a light to be turned on and seeing him—the car was a small secluded room where she was safe. But now? What if he came? He could go straight into the garage, take the car and drive to the police station, or out in the streets looking for her if he thought she had got out of the house. Follow her and hunt for her, letting the headlights scan the streets. . . .

She could see herself running in the streets, barefooted and her nightdress flapping, nowhere to hide while he came nearer in the car, the headlight shining right in her face when she turned round—and how he speeded up the car and made it run her down like a rhinoceros, and her legs got broken and the blood. . . . Nonsense. She was not in the streets, she was at home, lying in the car. She'd have to get away from here. Find out where he was. He would soon realise that she wasn't in the house and then there would be only one possibility; he'd come to the garage to get the car or to look for her here, that was if he didn't go back to bed.

Pull the covers over his head and go to sleep. No, he wouldn't do that, not after the way he had chased her, he wouldn't be able to sleep but would lie there staring into the dark, waiting for her to return, not daring even to breathe for fear of her. No, it wasn't credible that he would go back to bed. He couldn't lock the door, wouldn't dare sleep on the top floor; what if she came back and set the whole house on fire, that would have been something, burning him to death, properly, nothing like that little bed fire she had tried; but she was like that, couldn't bear thinking of violence if there was an easier way out, and the way she had done it he had, after all, been able to manage; she had given him a fair chance. He'd never do that to her, he was so hard, he would never give her an opportunity to get away. . . .

Where was he now? Could she hear him? Was he on

his way here? Sneaking silently down the basement stairs? God, here she was lying in the car, was she out of her mind? It was the most dangerous place in the whole house, what had she been thinking about? She thought she heard his footsteps but didn't know whether it was only the roaring in her ears that made her think so; if only he didn't come in while she was lying there. She must get out! Where? Where? God, if she went out of here she would meet him!

She knelt on the floor of the car and peered into the dark garage. She couldn't see very clearly but knew that there were some tools by one of the walls—he kept his garden tools here, rakes and spades, and there was a wheelbarrow too. She'd have to get over to the wheelbarrow. If it stood resting against the wall like wheelbarrows normally do then she could creep in between it and the wall and hide there so that he couldn't see her if he turned on the light.

Oh, if only he'd come! If only she could get it over and done with! He would see that she wasn't here, take the car and drive away, or go up to bed again and leave her free to slip out and fetch her coat and get down here again without having to dread his arrival and think of ways of escape. It wasn't too late yet. She could get dressed and go down to the station and take the train to her Mother's.

She opened the car door silently and slid across the floor to disappear among the shadows by the wall.

34

HE WAS still laughing as he walked down the basement stairs. *Ha, ha, little woman, I've come to get you now.* He had lost her at one point and been frightened when he didn't know where she was and couldn't be sure that she wasn't standing in some dark corner, waiting for him with something sharp in her hand. She hadn't been in the kitchen, but she could have gone into the living room, got hold of a vase or a lampstand, stood pressed against the wall and just waited for him to come in there and look for her. It had been terrifying for a moment and he had stayed in the kitchen with the light on, listening to her footsteps. But she wasn't on the ground floor and she couldn't have gone out of the front door either, for in that case she would have had to pass the open kitchen door where he was standing, and he would have seen her. She wasn't down here, or if she was then her heaving and sobbing had stopped completely.

A small chill of excitement went through him. What if she had fallen down dead? It wasn't impossible that he could have frightened her to death, made her fall down dead of sheer unadulterated fright. Perfect! Perfect! He hadn't used force, no one would be able to find anything. 'Heart attack. Unfortunately she was a little weak and probably thought she heard somebody down there and when she went down to have a look, she had been so very afraid of finding a stranger there that she had collapsed and just died. She had been a little nervous lately.' The cause of death was obvious, no signs of violence, she had just died, just like that. 'The remains of the fire up there? Oh, that was only me smoking in bed, that had nothing to do with her, we sleep in separate rooms and I haven't seen her since we said good-night last night.'

Perhaps she was dead. Perhaps she was lying out there in the living room and he'd just have to wait for a little while till he was sure that she wasn't breathing at all; then he could go round looking for her, turn on the lights everywhere before he went into each room, just stick his hand out and turn it on, so that she wouldn't have a chance to hit him, in case, against all the odds, she should be standing somewhere waiting for him. If she were dead, then he could simply laugh and be happy and wait till tomorrow when he could send for the doctor. If she wasn't there . . . well, there was she then? Not upstairs. Not outside. In the basement! She must be in the basement.

Instead of disappointment he felt a certain amount of relief. Oh no, had she been dead, it would have been far too easy, no, my little wife, you won't get away with it so easily. Now he hoped that she wouldn't be dead, how cheated he would have felt, what terrible mockery to find her dead body and know that he wouldn't be able to frighten her any more, not see her properly punished for what she had done to him tonight. He turned the light on everywhere on the ground floor but she wasn't there. Damn it! She had fooled him again after all, got away. You devil! Surely she wouldn't have opened the door to the garage and gone out that way?

No, he would have heard it, and for God's sake, she couldn't have gone out in the middle of the night barefoot and in her thin nightdress! That would have been a sight for the gods, in the light of the street lamps; but it was too much to hope for, the bitch was far too prudish; not even to save her own life would she go out in that state. Where would she go anyway? She couldn't go anywhere in that state. Least of all to the police, and the neighbours would die laughing if they saw her like that. Or they might come back with her if she played it really well and sobbed and screamed. They might believe her if she said she had run away because he was chasing her. Or believe.... Damn. God knows. He might be able to get her put in a mental home. In any case he'd have to go down to the basement now and have a look for her there.

He sneaked forward in the silent basement, trying to glide as quietly as possible, straining his ears to hear if she was there. She wouldn't be able to be absolutely quiet. She would at least have to breathe. Where could she have hidden? The boiler-room, the store room, the laundry room, the empty room? Not the empty room, she wouldn't be there, too easy to get to her there. She wasn't in the store room nor in the potato bin either. He began to feel slightly disturbed and uneasy; found himself looking over his shoulder, or standing still to listen after each step. Where was she? She must be somewhere. She must be down here in the basement. He wanted to turn the light on but was afraid of doing so; afraid to see her standing very near, white-faced and with burning eyes, and with something hard and heavy in her hands. He could hardly hear anything any more because of his own heavy breathing.

He suppressed a sudden wild impulse to call her: 'Yoohoo! Where are you?' and was forced to bite his lips in order not to let the words out.

Where was she, where was she? Not in the boiler-room, nor in the laundry room; yet he couldn't be sure, she might be in there, have been there all the time, standing behind the door while he looked in. He was afraid in the dark cellar and wanted to get away from there, up to bed, pull the covers over his head and just sleep. If only all this was over and done with, if only he could lie down and sleep and not have to run about in the middle of the night catching a cold just because of her idiotic idea. . . . He ought to have had her taken care of long ago. The woman was dangerous to herself as well as to others.

Then his glance fell on the garage door and at the same moment he saw through the frosted glass something that looked like a shadow moving across the room.

His good mood returned and he smiled with relief.

35

SHE ALMOST screamed when the door opened and the footsteps came into the garage.... No, not now. Oh, no, it mustn't be like that. He mustn't come. Not now. No, dear God. She had just found a place, a small, quiet place where she wouldn't be found. She couldn't be seen or heard, was doing nobody any harm—so that not even her breathing should betray her she had bitten so hard into her hand that the pain went through her whole arm. Not now. It wasn't fair. Not now that she had managed for so long, when she had almost outwitted him. It wasn't right. It would be the wrong finish to the whole affair if he came and found her now, kicked the wheelbarrow over and stood there looking down at her, laughing.

What would she do? She dared not think of it. She couldn't even think one minute ahead; what paralysed her thoughts was the fact that now, at this moment, she sat hiding behind the wheelbarrow and was safe. If he just turned the light on he would see her. There wasn't enough room for all of her behind it. She was sure that her hair was sticking up but dared not raise a hand to flatten it—the hand would shine white in the dark. And she couldn't curl up tighter without pushing the wheelbarrow out of its present position. No. Let him go away again. I'll be good. I must go on living. Must get away from him. Make up for all this in some way, perhaps. I could make him listen to my side of the story. Then I can go and live with Mother and get a divorce, he wouldn't object. . . .

Furtive steps across the floor. She heard his breathing now. At least he wasn't an animal; animals can smell their way to the prey but he had only his eyes to rely on. As long as he didn't turn the light on. . . .

She closed her eyes and bit her hand even harder; the light was on. Cold and hard it shone on the concrete walls, the garden tools, the car, the wheelbarrow with . . . instinctively she tried to shrink even more, it almost felt as though she had pulled her legs up into her body, but it was futile, he would see her just the same. It would be better just to come out and ask him why he was chasing her this way, what he meant by treating his own wife like that, was he mad? Or just get out and laugh and say, 'Now we'll stop all this, my friend, it was nice as long as it lasted but you and I are too old for this sort of game.' She'd have to do something, something had to happen, otherwise she'd fall against the wheelbarrow and it would turn over and reveal her on the floor like a bundled parcel at his feet; all her muscles were about to go into cramps and twitches; if she didn't get up from this squatting position she might even become an invalid and never be able to walk again.

She couldn't see him, but heard him walking over the floor determinedly. He didn't seem to have looked in her direction yet. She heard him chuckling and muttering to himself. Surely he couldn't think that she had gone out? No, for then he wouldn't be laughing like this, relieved, like at a nice secret. He must have searched through the house and know that she wasn't up there. He must know that she was here, somewhere

here in the garage. But why didn't he come? Was it the cat's game with the mouse, was he thinking of making her come out if he waited long enough? Was he going to sit there chuckling and sniggering till she came out of her own accord? She'd have to get hold of something . . . there were some spades by the wheelbarrow not far from her. If only she could stretch out an arm and get hold of one, unnoticed . . . or take hold of it quickly and then just rush forward. . . .

He was by the car now, had opened the door. A small shriek rose in her throat, a shriek that didn't get out through her mouth but went up into her head and stayed there, thundering. If she had stayed in the car! If she had still been in the car! If she had still been lying on the back seat! He sat down in the car now. Perhaps she could get away while he sat bending over the dashboard. . . . No. Wait. Just for a while. He was sitting in the car and she heard him starting it. He would leave. She took her hand away from her mouth and almost began to laugh loudly, the squeak from her brain slipped out through her mouth, but he couldn't have heard it because of the noise from the car engine. She wanted to laugh and jump. Idiot! Pig! I've cheated you, for the umpteenth time I've hoodwinked you, you peasant, you simple-minded idiot. I knew you'd never be able to get me. Giggling rose in her like air-bubbles in a straw, came out of her everywhere, through the ears, under her arms . . . oh, yes, go out and look for me in the streets, go, go, never come back any more; when you do come I'll be far from here.

The engine was running now, but the car was still not moving. He must be thinking hard, be about to decide on something. Well, soon he'd be gone.

Or had he changed his mind? Had he discovered that she was here? Had she let a sound escape her, shown her hair too much, stuck a leg out? He walked over to the garage door and felt it. Ah, he'd open it now, that was what he had forgotten, and now he'd go. Hurry, you nit, hurry, I can't sit like this much longer, you must go soon! But now his steps came back, and again she had to shrink and minimise her body so that he wouldn't see her when he walked across the floor. He was standing by the door to the stairs now, and turned off the light.

"Good night then, little wife," he said loudly and his voice was thick with laughter. "Good night and sleep well."

He walked out through the door and she heard him lock it behind him.

36

WITH A sigh he sat down on the bed, and now exhaustion came over him like a blanket, wrapped around him so that not even his head was free. He fell full length on the bed with his eyes closed. Sleep. Sleep now. A long, long sleep. Not to wake till it was light outside with the birds singing, a clean, light, new day. Dew on the grass and flowers in bloom. Alone in the house. The end of all this. Oh, God, to be able to breathe again. *Alone.* Clean, fresh, young and alone. Gone the rotting corpse and the grinding voice, gone the cunning eyes and sidelong glances, of the being that sneaked around all over the house and wanted to do him harm, that set traps, breathed a stink through the walls . . . it had been like living with a ghost, an evil spirit that wouldn't leave him in peace and that he couldn't get rid of, worse than a nightmare, for a nightmare finishes when you wake up again, and that was what he must do now, wake up! Fill his lungs with clean, fresh air and sing in the bathroom and make his own coffee. Buy a new suit and go out into the streets and meet lovely girls and come home when he felt like it. Get hold of somebody to clean the windows. Be free. His burden and his fear gone forever.

He would have to go down there some time tomorrow, of course, and he'd have to get rid of the burnt sheets. They would complicate the situation too much and wouldn't make it easier for him. He must get rid of them. Forget everything. He wouldn't be sorry but he might mourn her memory, remember the good things they had shared once, one mustn't speak ill of the dead. He wouldn't talk about what she had tried to do the last few days. 'Yes, she had been nervous and uneasy of late.' That was true, but she had tried to avoid him. He wouldn't mention what had happened—from now on it was forgotten and forgiven.

Perhaps he would let them find her scrap-book. 'Yes, that, well that isn't nice; I knew that she was fiddling with something, but what it was I didn't know. Was she that far gone? . . . if only I had known I could have helped her.' He would have to act terrified when he got down to the garage, and he mustn't forget the letter, of course. He would put that on the front of the car and put some little thing on top so it couldn't fall down. He would have to lift her from where she was lying and put her fingerprints in the car, so that it would look as though she really had been there herself! Of course, she couldn't drive a car but she had seen him starting it plenty of times, she always used to sit next to him. Obviously she must have taken notice. And when the problems had grown too big for her she had remembered. He couldn't have known.

It was she who had insisted that they sleep in separate rooms. He had asked her to stay in the bedroom with him, had been worried and wanted her to see a doctor. But she had been terribly stubborn and after all he couldn't force her. How was he to know? He himself hadn't been feeling too good lately, had taken a few sleeping tablets and fallen asleep almost immediately. And when he had woken later and not found her in her

144

room. . . . The terrible shock when he came into the garage, he hadn't believed his eyes at first. He had thought that she had been sleep-walking and fallen down there. He had tried to wake her but after a while he'd realised what had happened, that it was no longer possible to wake her, then he had seen the letter and read it. Only, he didn't really understand how it could have come to that; he had always thought they had been a happy couple. Of course they had had disagreements but what married couple doesn't? He had had no idea that it had been so hard on her.

He sighed, rubbed his cheek against the pillow, it was warm and soft, like a woman's bosom. Mmmmm. Young, firm, soft, lithe. Soon it would come true . . . another woman. Another woman. He would find a hard nipple where he now only had the pillow, which his head fell deeper into. Soon . . . if only it were already tomorrow. . . .

37

SHE DIDN'T understand. Didn't know what had happened. He had gone but she didn't know for how long. Had he just gone to get something? Would he be back soon? Should she dare get up and stretch her legs? For a few minutes it would be all right, he couldn't get back in a minute. Perhaps he had gone to have a pee. She giggled. At least he had meant to go out in the car. He had started it already and it was standing there humming. And if he had unlocked the garage door she could get out. She had been frightened stiff before when thinking about it while she was lying behind the barrow. Hadn't even been up to see if the key was in the door. But she knew that he used to put it in his pocket when he had locked it; he had the garage key on his key ring. But he'd been fiddling with the door. Had he unlocked it to be able to get out quickly when he returned? But why had he said good night, as though he knew she was in there? Why hadn't he searched for her then? Why hadn't he seen her?

Her head was swimming, and she was forced to sit down on the car and rest for a moment, stretch her arm and legs, breathe deeply. Idiotic to sit there, of course, she'd have to get out before he came back. Hide in the garden while he drove out and then go back indoors the same way and get dressed. Strangely simple it all seemed, he had even made it easier for her. How stupid he was. Or was he being clever? Was this what he had intended? She hid her face in her hands when the thought suddenly hit her that he might have forgiven her and so given her a chance to get out. He might have meant it *nicely* when he said good night. It was too peculiar and she couldn't think of a reason why it should be so—but suddenly it seemed possible and she grasped the possibility with both hands and held it tight. He *had* forgiven her. He had realised that she hadn't meant so badly after all, that she had only been angry and nervous and afraid, and thought ill of him because she thought he had given her the sleeping tablets (what if he had simply wanted her to have a good night's sleep, had just done it out of kindness?).

And he had woken up and seen what she had done and had naturally been furious, but then he had thought it over and understood how she must have felt, and he had hunted and frightened her to punish her but later he had forgiven her. She wanted to cry. She wanted to go up to him and say, 'Darling, thank you; please forgive me, you are too good to me, my dear. Next week we'll go on holiday like you said and I'll be good to you and you can smoke if you like'—no, not smoke, that wouldn't be a particularly happy topic to bring up —'but you needn't wipe your feet, and of course you can have a drink when you want it, and you know what? I'll clean the windows!' She rubbed her hands over her face and felt tears on her fingers; she wouldn't be able to undo anything but she would make an effort to change now, maybe it had been all to the good that the air had been cleared, they had both got rid of all their bad temper, they could make a fresh start, free and clean.

It felt so wonderful just sitting here waiting for him to come back, then she would walk up to him and . . . or should she sleep first? She was so tired. Her head felt so heavy. She hadn't slept yet tonight and it must be late now and they had been rushing madly about all night. At their age one can't carry on like that for very long . . . she wanted to rest for a while first. He'd no doubt wake her when he came back; carry her upstairs and put her to bed and perhaps take off her nightdress; she'd let him, she felt her thighs trembling already— they would seal their new-found understanding. He'd take her and she would lie on the bed and receive him. . . .

So tired. So tired. And a strange feeling in her head, as though she was drunk, yet that small glass of port surely couldn't have had any effect at all. And the atmosphere was strange . . . it was like a dream, something whispered in her head, something in the air she sensed. And the car, humming underneath her, it was as though it was far away, yet she was sitting right on top of it. . . . A peculiar weight in the air, something that was pressing her down. . . . It wouldn't matter if she opened the garage door. She could stay and wait for him just the same. Just open the door a little and get some fresh air. There was something unhealthy, something oily about the air in the garage, as though it contained some kind of gas. . . . She got up and took a few steps towards the garage door, felt her legs collapsing under her so that she suddenly found herself kneeling—it was like walking in deep water, or like a dream when one is running yet doesn't move an inch, something held her back . . . and this peculiar air. There was something in it that she hadn't felt earlier. If only she

148

knew where it was coming from. She clung to the wall as she struggled towards the door, fumbled to get hold of the handle, found it, and pressed and twisted it, but nothing happened.

So he hadn't unlocked it. But the key, maybe he had left that in the lock? No! No key! Locked! And the door to the basement he had locked when he left. He had locked her in. And he had been gone for so long now it was as though he didn't intend to come back. He had locked her in and she couldn't work out why. And what was in the atmosphere, what was it that made it so difficult for her to breathe and seemed to be stifling her?

She stood pressing her forehead against the wall in an attempt to think more clearly. But it only came nearer—this something. And the car that just stood there humming away without moving at all . . . why didn't he come and turn the engine off?

Then she felt ice cold. She knew now. She turned to face the room and screamed. She screamed, not for help for she knew that he wouldn't come and help her and that he wouldn't even be able to hear her, but in anger and hate and horror, shouting foul words which she had never uttered before, she stamped and jumped on the floor. *Devil. . . . Filthy bastard. . . .* She cursed and sobbed wildly, tore her hair, spat on the floor.

Then she ran blindly across the garage, up to the small window in the corner of the wall, and fought with stiff fingers to open it.

38

SHE LAY in a huddle outside on the grass—somehow
she must have managed to get out there, through the
tiny garage window, but she didn't recall how. Her
hands and legs were bleeding, she tasted blood in her
mouth and there was a pain in her head that grew
stronger and stronger every minute; she screamed but
couldn't drown it. There were stars too, which seemed
to turn around, but they were real stars for she knew
she was lying on the cold, wet grass outside the garage
looking up at the pitch-black sky and the stars. She
couldn't move, she just lay in a heap on the grass with
her mouth full of blood. Hatred so powerful that it
swelled and boiled inside her left her helpless. She
couldn't get up. She couldn't manage to run any longer
but knew she'd have to flee before he came. Flee. Bleeding and in a torn nightdress and with this exasperating
pain in her head that drowned all thought. There was
no way out.

Only one way, and that was the one that led into his
bedroom. But all the doors in the house were locked—
she couldn't get in. The garage window was open. No,
there were gases in there, lethal gases. He had tried to
murder her and it had been deliberate this time—no
joke; he had turned on the car engine and the gases
were to have killed her. And he had left, laughing,
nothing could help her any more, not Mother, not

God, not the police, nothing. The only thing that would kill the pain in her head would be to see him dead.

He would come to the garage in the morning and see that she wasn't there. He would fling the garage window open and know that he'd have to look for her. . . . She mustn't be here then. She would have to be somewhere where she could get at him, but where he couldn't see her. She'd have to get into the garage again. Get a knife from the kitchen and go up to his room. It didn't matter any more if they came and took her away afterwards; it didn't matter if she was put in jail. If only she could pull out his eyes and cut his tongue off.

If only she had known what to do about the car. But when she had realised what was happening in the garage she had been so overwhelmed by horror that she hadn't dared to think or even look in the car. She wouldn't have known what to do or what to turn off, but if only she had been more cool-headed and less frightened she could have taken her time to have a look and work out for herself how to do it.

The garage was the only place she could wait for him. Out here in the garden, alone and defenceless, she would be done for. When he came, he'd catch her or chase her screaming into the street; at any rate he would catch up with her sooner or later, and she would miss the greatest moment in her life, the moment when she turned on him and ran the knife into his face. She'd have to get back to the garage. She was lying on the ground with bleeding knees telling herself: You must get back into the garage. You must get hold of a spade, hide behind the car and when he comes, get up and just hit, hit, hit, hit—before he has a chance to think and realise what's happening.

151

She must get back into the garage, she must turn off the engine. But how could she? The lethal gases in there might force her to her knees again and kill her before she could do anything ... still, it was the only way, she must get back into the garage and have something hard in her hand when he came back. If only she could manage to get in and stand by the window, breathing fresh air till he came ... she'd have to leave the car, leave the engine running. But if she could just keep her face turned towards the window, she would manage.

It would be morning soon. The sky would get lighter and change to purple and then blue. He would wake up and come down, laughing contentedly, but he wouldn't find her where he expected. When she heard him on the stairs, she could go and hide behind the door and when he came in bash him on the back of his head first of all so that he fell forward—and then stand over him, laughing while he fought to get up. Perhaps leave him down there with his exhaust fumes? Go up and have a wash and get dressed and later come down and find him? 'Oh, no, how tragic, he must have fallen and knocked himself unconscious after he had started the car engine.' An accident, it would look like an accident. . . .

39

HE WOKE up and knew that something awaited him, something he must do. Something important. He felt calm when he woke. It wasn't like the usual damned feeling of having to get up yet again, everything still dark as midnight and the wife standing there with her sour night-smell about her, sweaty sheets, a grinding feeling of discomfort that sometimes didn't ease off till the middle of the day. . . . It felt different now. Mild. Warm. He wanted to smile even before he was properly awake. The sunshine falling into the room coloured the inside of his eyelids pink. He stretched out on the bed. There was a wonderful warmth all around. He wanted to turn on to his other side and go to sleep again, but not really sleep, just lie there quiet and warm and let the thoughts go idly through his head. Strong coffee. Go fishing. It must be Saturday today. Football. Shout himself hoarse. Laugh. Eat a good dinner out. Go out dancing. Sit at a table and listen to the music and ask pretty girls to dance, press himself against them, drink good whisky, tell stories. . . .

The house was still and silent. He sensed that he was alone, that she was no longer breathing all over him, that her heaving breath and rough voice, her shuffling slippers, were gone, gone. . . . He still hadn't captured the thought he knew was lurking in his head, and which would in time emerge, the thought of where she was. He didn't want to think about that now. She could have gone away. He didn't think she was still asleep; no, she was more distant than that, her presence was gone from the house, otherwise he would have sensed it in the air. Her smell was gone. Her bed was empty. The window was open now and fresh air was pouring in. . . . A bird was singing, the sun was shining. Get dressed in a while. Perhaps have a bath, go down and make breakfast, out to the garage and take the car and. . . .

The garage.

The garage. Something was crawling up his spine now. Something that wanted to get into his head. It had something to do with the garage.

Then he saw the picture before him; the dark house, the light burning in the garage, how he had started the engine, heard her heavy breathing, heard how she sniffed the snot back up into her nose. Heard his own laughter.

Was it a dream? Was it a dream that he had been chasing her through the house and had trapped her in the garage, or was *this* a dream of waking on a sunny morning, with the air so strong and clear that he felt good, felt that he had slept long enough, felt happy and exhilarated, and that in a while he would drive into the country, taking his lunch and. . . . He wanted to sleep again. Do everything differently. Wake up again a little later and know the truth. He didn't really want to know it yet. Everything had been so wonderful when he woke, his whole body had felt good.

He needed more sleep. He couldn't really manage to get up yet and find out what had really happened. What if she was lying there. If he were to find her lying dead on the floor, the air thick and heavy, he would

154

have to start screaming, and shouting, and call for help and cry and blame himself. Well, he hadn't wanted to get involved in a lot of nonsense again, a lot of questions and squabbling. Wasn't that why he had done it? To avoid more quarrels? To be left in peace? To protect himself and have a bit of peace and quiet? If only he could go to the garage and find it empty apart from the car. If only she were gone. Vanished. Anything. If only he wouldn't have to see her. If only he could stop thinking about her altogether. If only he could be left in peace.

He sat up in bed and tried to decide. On the floor was an ashtray with several cigarette stubs. In the sheet was a huge burnt hole. He remembered. He knew what had happened last night.

He no longer wanted to lie down and sleep. He must get this over and done with, get the whole business out of the way as soon as possible. Get her out of the garage, get someone to come and cope with her. He couldn't live like this with her in the garage, dead. He covered his face with his hands and sat like that for a while, absolutely still. No, he wouldn't cry. He didn't want to cry. It wasn't her he was crying about, because she was dead, but all that she had spoiled between them. All the kind thoughts, the friendly feelings that had been and now were dead, that was what he mourned. Not her. He was happy to be rid of her. But he must get her out. He must turn off the car engine. He must get people to come, and he'd have to scream and cry for a time till it was all over, so that they could take her away, take away all the horrible things she had become, leave him alone with the good things that had existed and that still existed in him.

He mustn't be sorry now. It wasn't murder. You couldn't call it murder. He hadn't even touched her. It was her own fault. He couldn't have known that she was in there. If only she had come out. If only she hadn't put burning cigarettes in his bed. He had meant well, after all. Yesterday evening. He had taken his sleeping tablets and gone to bed, to sleep. Not even thought about doing her any harm. Just wanted to sleep, had been so tired. It was only because she had started fiddling about, that it had happened. If only she had been a little nicer. . . .

He'd have to go down there. He'd have to get it over and done with. It wouldn't help if he lay down and went to sleep again for sooner or later he'd have to get up and look for her in the house—and finally find her in the garage. It was unavoidable and he could decide himself when he wanted to do it. He couldn't just leave it. The sooner he did it the better.

He knew there was a letter somewhere that he'd have to take with him and put beside her where it would be seen. He was tired, couldn't think straight any more. A letter would have to be found by her side. It would have to have been her who had started the car—not him. He would have to arrange it with fingerprints. He would have to touch her. A wave of disgust went through him at the thought that she might not be dead yet. What if she were breathing, what if she moved when he took hold of her, if she woke up and gazed at him with hard, light blue eyes, if she opened her mouth and said something? What if she wasn't dead? He started to shudder and tried vainly to keep still so that he could listen properly. Maybe she was sneaking about the house again! What if she had got out somehow! Suppose she were still alive! If she had already planned her revenge! But no, she must still be down in the garage—both the garage door, the basement door and the outer door were locked and he had the keys. She must still be there. But if she wasn't really dead yet. . . . If she woke up and moved and started to scream and hit him!

He wanted to creep down into bed again and pull the bedclothes over his head; lie with his hands pressed over his face and not think, just lie there. He'd have to go and look. He must! He would die of fright if she moved and looked at him. He'd have to take something with him to make sure that she was done for, dead, unable to spoil anything else any more. He must have something. A cloth to put over her head just in case. Just put it loosely to make sure nobody would be able to say that he had suffocated her. It would be doing her a favour—finishing her off, stopping her sufferings. After all, nothing would ever be the same as before. It would be better to spare her the burden of her guilt by letting her die! Or should he take something hard; if she was breathing a cloth could fall off—it ought to be something harder in any case. He must have something in his hand!

He went down the stairs and into the living room and found a heavy glass ashtray, and with that in his hand he walked down the stairs to the basement.

40

FINISHED.

Finished. It is finished.

God, my whole body is shaking. I'm shaking as though I've done something, as though something terrible has happened.

Nothing has happened. Nothing. No, no! I'm standing in front of the mirror leaning heavily against the table and I can see my own wide-open eyes—no. They can't be my eyes. Not my face. I don't look like that. It isn't me. I once saw a film in the cinema about someone who went mad and looked like this. The face just as pale and stiff as mine, deep lines in it, shadows, blue rings around the eyes, just like this. And the eyes were staring, hard, expressionless. As though they were afraid of something. As though they thought that someone was going to come from behind, sneaking across the floor, holding something, coming nearer and nearer. . . .

No. No. Don't hit. Don't hit me. No! No, it was nothing. It was nobody. I am here alone. There's only me in the whole house. I'm lying on the floor, on the mattress in front of the chest-of-drawers, my hands are clasped around my neck as though to protect my head. I can hear myself crying and I feel that my face is wet and I think I've vomited a little on the floor.

I'm lying on the floor by the chest-of-drawers, vomit-

158

ing and crying. I. I who should have been laughing
and singing, rejoicing and clapping my hands. God,
what's the matter with me. I am happy now, aren't I?
I am glad now, aren't I? I must laugh, hahaha! For
Christ's sake, I'm free now. Free, I saw it myself, I'm free!
    It wasn't me who did it. It wasn't my fault. I didn't
mean to. It just happened and I don't know how. I just
stood there and then suddenly we were facing each
other, looking one another in the eye—and something
had gone too far, there was no way back, only the one
solution. It wouldn't have done just to hold out our
hands, empty and open, to have taken each others'
hands and said, 'What has happened? We must have
both gone mad; surely we should be able to live
together again like we did before.' But it was too late
then. One of us had to die. If I hadn't hit first I should
have been lying there now, it was self-defence. It wasn't
my fault. I couldn't help it. I would never have done
it if I hadn't known that if I hadn't done it then. . . .
    I can't believe it. No! no! It isn't true. It only
happened in a dream or in my head. I must be mistaken.
It can't be true. The corpse, the corpse that lay there,
blood streaming out of a hole in the head and the pool
on the floor that grew bigger and bigger. The horrible
sound when the skull broke. No, good God, no, it can't
be true. I couldn't have done a thing like that! Yes, it's
true that I've been toying with the idea of poison, and
inexplicable accidents and strange diseases. But not
blood! Never blood! Not a broken head and a pair of—
eyes that stared at me like that. Blood that came out of
the mouth instead of words which would have come, if
I'd waited a little while. . . .
    I nearly fell to my knees on the garage floor and cried

159

and begged forgiveness. Sorry, sorry, sorry, I didn't mean to hurt you, I have never wanted to hurt you; it isn't my fault that everything went wrong, I never wanted it to. I only wanted us to be friends. All the time I wanted us to like each other, for everything to be pleasant. It was you who spoiled it all. It was your own fault. You started the trouble. It wasn't I who wanted it like that! I didn't start it!

But when I saw the body lying there, it seemed as though the fault was mine, too. After all, it was I who struck first. I could have waited instead, could have let myself be hit or dodged the blow that was aimed at me. Perhaps it would never have come? I'll never know. Perhaps I was the most horrible, the most evil and relentless of the two of us. It was me. After all, it was me who killed.

It's over now. The house is mine. I'm here alone. I shan't hear any angry voices, nobody will come and upset me, there'll be no quarrels, no humiliations. Silence. I get up from the floor. I won't think about it just now. I'll wait till they come, till they find what they must find. Until then I'll be alone in the silent house, enjoy the peace and the blissful calm for a couple of days, perhaps for a couple of hours only. The peace I've longed for and looked forward to enjoying for so many years. I get up, but I don't look in the mirror this time. I'm afraid of what I'll see there. That horrible face that isn't mine, staring at me. And the horror of something that might appear behind me, something . . . laughing insanely—rushing through the air and throwing itself over me with sharp claws that tear and rip and scratch out my eyes. I look straight forward. I walk into the garden. Out into the sun. I'm thinking about nothing.

160